I0722278

© 2023 Phoenix Blackwood

Phoenix Blackwood
The Love that Binds Us

All rights reserved. No part of this publication may be reproduced, stored in a retrieval system or transmitted in any form or by any means, electronic, mechanical, photocopying, recording or otherwise without the prior permission of the copyright holder.

Published by: Cinnabar Moth Publishing LLC
Santa Fe, New Mexico

Cover Design by: Ira Geneve

ISBN-13: 978-1-953971-69-2
Library of Congress Control Number: 2022949280

The Love that Binds Us

PHOENIX BLACKWOOD

Dedication:

To those of you who feel alone or too broken to be loved -- you're perfect. Keep fighting and love will come.

Content Notes:

The Love that Binds Us deals with many difficult topics that may be triggering for some readers.

Drug use (explicit)
Explicit language
Child abuse (non-sexual, explicit)
Medical trauma (explicit)
Genitalia mutilation (implied)
Homophobia (explicit)

INTRO

The term "broken family" implies that there was something whole to begin with. While mine might've appeared whole to the outside eye looking in, it was anything but. Sure, there was a mom and a dad, with two kids – the picturesque Christian American family. What they didn't see was the shouting, the arguments about how my father was a "bad example" or failed to uphold his "godly" duties to the family. Even in the passing moments that weren't arguments, there was a constant tension that could be cut with a knife. Passive-aggressive facial expressions, disapproval of how things were handled by the other party.

As the oldest of the two kids, all this tension fell directly on my shoulders. I loved my dad to death. He was always the one to console me when I was upset, bring me home ice cream, and purposely take time out of his day just to spend it with my sister and I. He was the one who went out of his way to teach me sign language so that I could communicate better with my sister, who was born deaf. My mom had opted out of cochlear implants because Leah was born "as she was meant to be." She wouldn't even consider a surgery that would give her daughter the ability to hear. Countless arguments centered around just that – dad wanted her to have the surgery, but he couldn't outwill my mother. Personally, I think Leah should have been consulted in all this, as it was her body. When Leah was six, she asked if there was any way for her to be able to hear. Dad slept on the couch for the next week because my mother said he'd "put the idea in her head."

When I turned thirteen, dad had had enough. He packed up in the night, was gone in the morning, and I haven't seen him since. He left a note telling me how much he loved my sister and I, and that his leaving had nothing to do with us. I brought the note to my mother, tears streaming down my face, and asked her why she made him leave. For the first time in my life, she struck me across the face. I walked away, still crying, and hid in my room for the next two days, refusing to come out even for food. I never told anyone she'd hit me, but to know she had that power within her lingered in the back of my head for years. I'd lost one of the most important people in my life, and didn't know if I'd ever see him again, and my mother's response was violence. I lost my trust in both parents on the same day.

I'd never gotten along well with my mother. I was never good enough in her eyes. Leah was the perfect child, and my mother held Leah on a pedestal while I slowly drowned in my emotions. I didn't resent Leah for this – it wasn't her fault our mother seemingly hated me. Leah was my one and only reason to stay in the house, instead of just running away to Theo's and throwing up the middle finger to my mother. I would go to the ends of the earth to make sure Leah was safe and cared for, and that she'd never know the coldness I received from our mother.

Theo. Theo kept me sane in everything. They had their struggles, and I knew I'd have to help them sometimes, but they were there for me in a way that no one else was. They'd never walk out because of my mother, and they would absolutely never lay a hand on me. They even taught themself some basic sign language so that they could communicate with my sister on the occasion they came to my house. They didn't come over often – my mom didn't like them. She'd turned her nose up the first day I'd brought them to my house when I was eleven, knowing that they'd been adopted by a single woman. I never understood it—as a Christian, aren't you supposed to want to help those in need, not exile them? My mom's "Christianity" was incredibly warped, only adhered to her strict mindset of what a family should look like. A single mother didn't fit this description, even though she eventually became one as well.

I defied her with this friendship. I'd defy her even more in the years to come.

CHAPTER ONE

Theo and I walked into the small frozen yogurt shop after a particularly long day at school. Things had calmed down a bit since Theo had come out and started transitioning. It had been a few months, and the initial heckling had died down. Most people at school didn't fuck with us anymore, but there was always that one group that would try and make us miserable if they had the chance. Theo had moved out of the class that they shared with that group, but this morning the tormentors waited in the hallway outside our first class of the day. They must've been bored, because they perked up at the chance to approach Theo and me. Pushing us apart, they started shoving Theo back into the lockers while corralling me away. They tried to touch me, and Theo reacted by ducking under arms to plow into the guy that had his hands aimed for my breasts. He fell, and we ran into the classroom before things had a chance to get seriously out of hand. The others didn't dare follow us—it was science class, and the teacher had a no-nonsense policy that would get them suspended quickly. However, the rest of the day we were on edge waiting for another assault.

Theo had gotten much better at containing the angry responses that rose up in them. I was proud of them, but there was still a limit, and I always got anxious when I could see them teetering on the edge. We tried to avoid confrontation as much as possible instead of setting them up to fall into bad situations all day. It was difficult either way—homophobia and transphobia ran rampant through the school—we were outsiders, sitting as far away from the general population in the cafeteria as we could. Jeremy would join us at times, but he was the only one.

We walked in the shop to get away for a minute, being transported to a colorful world of sweets and fun. It had become somewhat of a ritual. On bad days we'd get frozen yogurt topped with all kinds of candies. Theo always got chocolate with strawberry bubbles, and I would get whatever the special flavor of the week was with as many different kinds of chocolate candies as possible on top. We'd sit in the front of the store and watch all the people walking by. Today, we sat on stools at the counter in front of the window and gazed on as groups and families passed by.

"Al, look!" Theo pointed as a kid rode by on a unicycle. An unusual sight for the middle of the city, but not the strangest.

I laughed, "Imagine the tricks you could do on that." I tapped them on the shoulder with the back of my hand.

They rolled their eyes, "Hah, I'd fall flat on my ass in no time. I can barely ride a bike."

"You'd think with all the skateboarding you'd be able to!"

"For some reason I can't balance well when I'm sitting, I've gotta be standing."

I scraped the last of the cereal milk flavored yogurt out of my cup and put it in my mouth. The taste was sweet and slightly bitter at the same time, the warmth from my hands making it taste more like regular yogurt than frozen. I stuck my spoon in Theo's cup to steal some of the rich chocolate that they still had brimming over the sides.

They snorted, "Why do you always get a small and then mooch off of mine?"

"You eat so damn slow, I can't help it. Act like you'd finish it without my help anyway." I chuckled.

They relented and placed the cup on the counter between us, but not before taking another spoonful for themself. We finished the cup together, and then ventured out into the street. Sticking out much less here, we walked holding hands and didn't care who saw. Unlike school, most people walking had better things to do than pick on a queer couple unprompted.

"Wanna come over?" Theo asked as we made our way down the street.

"I can't, I've gotta be home to watch my little sister when she gets back at four. Shit, what time is it?"

Theo pulled out their phone and checked it. "3:45."

"Damn, I gotta hurry."

We continued walking together, albeit at a quicker pace. My house was one street over from Theo's, so we had the same route back regardless of which house we went to.

"Why don't you come over to my house? My mom won't be home until six. I'm sure Leah would love to see you."

They flashed a half-smile. "Sure."

We hurried down the street back to my house, making it home right as the bus was dropping my sister off. She ran up and hugged me when she got off the bus, and I unlocked the front door to let us all in.

"Liz!" She signed.

Leah didn't know about Theo's transition, or that we were dating. My mom couldn't know, she'd never let Theo in the house again, so we'd decided together not to tell Leah. Expecting her to keep such a secret was too much to put on an eight-year-old, so we decided it would be better if she didn't know at all.

Theo smiled and gave her a hug, gesturing towards her room for her to go and grab her Nintendo. She *adored* playing games with Theo. Theo hated to admit it, but they were absolutely awful at video games, meaning that Leah usually won. She never won when she played against me, and she always knew when I let her win. I grabbed a couple of bottles of water and flopped down on the couch, Leah nestled between me and Theo with a controller in her hands ready to go. They played for a while as I scrolled through social media on my phone.

After an hour, Leah had her fill and asked to watch television instead. We switched the TV back to cable for her and then retreated into my room. Being that I spent hardly any time here, my room was like a time capsule of my preteen years. Nothing had been touched since I was thirteen. My walls were pink, there were boy band posters covering half of them, and there were even horse figurines lining a shelf next to my closet. Though If I'm being honest, I still liked those.

I sat on my bed and pulled Theo down to my level, kissing them on the forehead. They sat down with me and kissed me on the lips until they were leaning over me and my hands were wrapped around the back of their neck, pulling them closer. They were so soft, always so tender. I focused all my attention on the kiss, so much so that I didn't hear the small squeak of my door opening. Theo pulled away suddenly, jarring me and forcing me to look in the direction of their gaze.

Leah had opened the door. She stood there with her mouth open, her face frozen in wonder and confusion. She'd known Theo since we'd become friends, I bet she had never imagined finding us kissing when she opened my door.

Theo and I looked at each other in horror. The secret was out, how were we going to get her to keep quiet? We should've been more careful. We'd gotten too comfortable.

I signed for Leah to come sit between us on the bed. My face got hot as she sat and tears brimmed in my eyes. My mom could never, ever find out – Leah knowing was *so* dangerous. She looked up at me with wide eyes and signed, "Boyfriend?"

Theo must've seen the panic rising up in me, because they took over. They gently rested one hand on her shoulder to get her attention and then explained. "We love each other. I'm not a boy, but I'm still her partner. I'm like a boyfriend, just minus the boy part."

It was the simplest explanation, and she understood instantly. She looked back at me with a grin showing her missing teeth and signed, "Liz is better than any boyfriend. I like her."

A tear forced its way out and rolled down my cheek. It was so simple to her, she was so accepting, she didn't even miss a beat.

She reached up and wiped away the tear, "Why are you sad?"

"Mom can't find out. She'd be angry."

"She'd be mad that Liz isn't a boy?"

"Yes."

"That's silly. Dad was a boy and that didn't work. Maybe it's better with girls?"

She got me with that one, a laugh forced its way out of my chest. It was hollow, but still a laugh nonetheless.

"You can't tell mom, okay?"

She crossed her heart. "Promise."

I wrapped her in a hug, and Theo leaned in, asking, "Since she knows, can I tell her?"

I nodded, turning Leah to face Theo again as they signed away.

"I'm not a boy, but I'm not a girl either. I'm neither. My name is Theo."

"Is that why you cut your hair?" Leah had always been drawn to Theo's previously long hair. She'd cried when they cut it.

"Yes, I like it better this way."

She looked back at me, "Should I not tell mom that either?"

"No, I don't think she'd let them come over anymore."

A somber expression overtook Leah's face, "I don't want that, I like when Theo comes over."

A grin cracked across Theo's face at her use of their name. I felt so bad having to hide them from my mom when the recognition made them so happy. At least they understood why we had to hide, they'd never questioned it.

Leah turned back to Theo and wrapped her arms around their waist in a quick hug before signing, "I'll call you Theo when mom's not around, okay?"

They smiled and nodded at her, ruffling her hair. She stood up from the bed and then looked back at the two of us, "Will you come watch TV with me, or do you want to kiss more?"

We all broke into laughter. A loud cackling from each of us. Theo was the first to get up and drag me by the arm to the couch where Leah sat between us and happily munched on some sugary cereal she'd gotten from the cupboard.

After about half an hour, a key turned in the lock and my mom walked through the door. She looked at us and immediately took the cereal out of Leah's hands.

"You'll spoil your dinner."

She glanced at Theo with a scowl. She'd been even less fond of them since their transition, though we acted like it didn't happen around her. I suspect that she still knew, but allowed them to exist so long as it wasn't mentioned.

"You should let your hair grow out, dear. It looks boyish."

Theo had recently gotten a trim on their hair, forming it back into a fauxhawk. The comment was a dig, and I could see the snark that Theo was holding back.

"Mom." I shot a glare at her, a disapproving tone backing my voice.

She raised her hands in defense but didn't apologize and took the cereal box to the kitchen. Theo got up from the couch.

"I should go."

I got up too. "I'll come."

"No, you won't," my mom called from the kitchen, "I've got plans after dinner, you need to be here to watch Leah."

"Fuck." I muttered.

"Excuse me?"

I sighed, "Nothing."

I gave Theo a hug since I couldn't kiss them with my mom here, and walked them to the exit. They gave me a weak smile before they turned to walk down the street and I closed the door. Turning back to the living room, I plopped down on the couch next to Leah again and pulled out my phone.

"I'm sorry." I texted Theo. I always felt like I had to apologize for my mother, she was insufferable towards them.

About twenty minutes later, mom called us into the dining room. Turning off the television, I ushered Leah in and we sat at the table, my mom at the head and Leah and I on either side. It was an acceptable dinner—chicken parmesan with spinach—but nothing compared to Theo's brother's cooking. I was spoiled from eating there so often. He could go on and be a chef without even finishing high school.

Mom turned to me as I picked at my dinner. "I'm not sure you should have Liz around here. That hair, the way she dresses, she might influence Leah. Are you sure she's not a dyke?"

"That's a hateful word, mom." I didn't even look up. I heard it enough at school.

"No matter what you call it, I don't want Leah around it."

"Leah loves her, mom. You really want to take that away because you *think* she might be gay?" Anger boiled beneath the surface. I did my best to keep it out of my voice.

"That's exactly the problem—if she likes her so much she'll be apt to copy her. Her sister hanging around with that kind of person might tell her it's okay to be like that."

I dropped my fork on the plate and let out an audible sigh. "Whatever, mom." Getting up, I grabbed my phone from the couch and went to my room. I hated this. I couldn't be around my mom for ten minutes without getting mad, we never got along. She'd never be able to get me to stop seeing Theo and she knew that, so she was trying to take control the only way she knew how—using Leah as a pawn.

I turned on my phone to see a text from Theo.

"Stop apologizing for things that aren't your fault. I love you, I'll see you tomorrow."

I sighed and held the phone to my chest, staring up at my ceiling. They were too forgiving, I just wished I didn't have to fight this battle with my mom every day. Today had been a close call, and now that Leah knew it was likely only a matter of time until my mom found out.

A rush of dread overtook my body, and I started shaking. If my mom acted like this now, with nothing but hunches, how would she react when everything was out in the open? What would she do to me, to Theo?

I pulled the blankets over me and curled up on my side, trying to shut out the thoughts. A while later, the familiar creak of my door sounded. I didn't turn around, assuming it was my mom looking in before leaving for whatever night she had planned. When the door closed again and I heard small footsteps approach, I turned over to see Leah. I turned on my bedside table lamp, as the room had grown dark since I'd been laying there.

"Mom doesn't like Theo, does she?" she signed.

She caught more from reading lips than my mother gave her credit for. She underestimated both of us.

I shook my head, the anxiety in my chest easing slightly as Leah crawled into bed with me.

"I promise I won't tell. I don't want her to make Theo go away."

Hugging her close, I kissed her on the top of the head. I let her use my phone to put some cartoons on, and ran my hands through her long, dirty-blond hair, easing out the tangles as my fingers caught on them. Eventually, she dropped my phone and fell asleep in my arms.

———————

The next day, Theo plopped next to me on the bus after we stopped at their house. After putting their bag down in front of them, they wrapped an arm around me and kissed me. Smiling, they pressed their forehead to mine.

"Good morning."

"Hey," I mumbled, reaching around their back and pulling them into a hug. They let me and wrapped their arms around my waist.

"What's wrong?" The concern edged into their words.

"I'm just… It's my mom. Last night she said that I shouldn't bring you around Leah anymore."

They pulled back. "Did Leah tell her?"

"No. She came into my room and promised again not to tell, she doesn't want our mom to get mad. Mom's just… she's just awful to you. I wish she wasn't like this. I'm so afraid of her finding out."

Theo sighed and rested their chin on the top of my head. "I wish you didn't have to worry. Why don't you come over tonight? We can just relax."

"Okay," I said, leaning into their chest.

We stayed like that until the bus arrived at school, then we got off and reluctantly entered the building, hoping that the hecklers had something better to do today.

They didn't.

In fact, they were waiting by Theo's locker. As Theo ignored them and went to unlock it, one of the boys slammed it shut just as Theo was opening it. They took in a deep breath through their nose, closing their eyes for a second. I drew closer to them, staring daggers at the boy, hoping he'd give up and their group would leave.

The boy gave Theo a hard shove and their eyes flew open, a familiar fire sparking in them that meant soon it would be too late for me to intervene.

The warning growl came from deep in their throat. "Leave us the fuck alone."

"Or what, you little bitch?" The kid had the audacity to laugh in their face.

I caught Theo's fist as it raised in the air and they were startled by the sudden resistance, and turned to look at me. The look in their eyes softened, and they took another deep breath. I could see them consider how badly they needed whatever was in their locker, and then decide it wasn't worth it. They took my hand gently and we started walking in the opposite direction of the group, towards our first classes.

I thought we were in the clear when suddenly I was yanked back by someone grabbing the top strap on my backpack. Theo stopped and turned around as their hand was jerked back by my sudden halt. The fire sprang back in their eyes; they'd had enough. They always reacted so much faster when it was me that people went after instead of them.

I didn't catch their fist this time, and it connected with the face of whichever boy was behind me. There was a yelp, and then a release of the grip on my bag. Then Theo took my hand again as if nothing had happened, and we walked on. Just like that, it was over. At least a single punch was enough to deter this one. Sometimes we weren't so lucky.

Truth be told, I had no idea how to fight. I spent most of my time trying to keep Theo calm and generally didn't worry about defending myself, because Theo would spring into action if it was really needed. Sometimes even if it wasn't. It really depended on the day, how far they could be pushed before there was a reaction. Thankfully, they'd gotten much better at taming their emotions and knew when to stop, so they usually left it at a warning shot that sent the bullies running with their tails between their legs. The bullies were lucky. Theo knew how to do so much worse if they really wanted to.

Theo walked me to my class, and we parted ways at the door. I sighed as I sat down at my desk, staring up at the blackboard where the teacher was writing a quote from the book we'd been assigned to read this week. My stomach hurt, probably from the stress of everything. I wished that I didn't have to fight my way through the day with every interaction, at home and at school. At least tonight I'd go over to Theo's, the one place I could truly relax. Theo's family was so accepting, no one judged us for existing there. I was welcomed with open arms and friendly smiles. I wasn't a "bad daughter" there, I wasn't failing to be pure enough for them.

———

Walking through the threshold of Theo's house was like a weight lifting off my shoulders, all the tension of home and school falling away. This was what home was supposed to feel like. I flopped down on the couch and Theo joined me a couple minutes later with two mugs of tea, handing me one. I leaned into them as they wrapped an arm around my shoulders after turning the television on to the latest show we'd been binging. This felt so safe, so calm. A feeling I rarely got in my own home. Always on edge, an internal dissonance telling me that I wasn't good enough. Here, I was everything I was supposed to be.

We watched television until Seth—Theo's brother—made his way down the stairs and started rummaging through the kitchen to start dinner. The house was quickly filled with smells that made my mouth water – meat searing in a pan, vegetables being chopped, pasta water boiling. I sat in the scents until I couldn't take it any longer and my stomach growled, causing me to get up and make my way into the kitchen.

Seth shot me a sly smile. "Probably another ten minutes."

I pouted, staring at the food and willing it to cook faster. Seth laughed when he looked up at me, tearing his attention from the stove and pointing to the silverware drawer.

"Hand me a fork."

I got one out and gave it to him, wondering why he needed a new one when there was already one sitting on the counter next to him. He stabbed the fork into a large mushroom in the frying pan, and then without looking handed it back to me. I grabbed it eagerly and took a bite. It was so savory that my mouth watered even more, a perfect mixture of herbs and spices hitting all the right notes. It burned my mouth a bit, but I didn't even care. The mushroom was gone within seconds, and I was left pacing between the kitchen and the living room while I waited for more. In the meantime, I got out four plates and sets of silverware and set them around the island in the kitchen, trying to make myself useful.

Theo appeared in the kitchen a minute later, setting their cup of tea next to one of the plates and my cup near theirs. I sat down next to them and waited eagerly as Seth started dishing out the food – mushroom and chicken alfredo. I dug in the second the food hit my plate, shoveling a forkful of the noodles in my mouth. It was a perfect mixture of creamy and salty, noodles tender but not overcooked. The chicken was perfectly seared and still juicy on the inside. I downed the entire thing before Theo was even halfway done with their plate. Seth hadn't even sat down yet. He'd made a plate for Monica—Theo's and his mom—and put it away in the fridge first. I guessed she wouldn't be home for a while.

Seth snickered at me before taking another helping of food and piling it onto my plate.

"Never be a food critic Alex. You've gotta actually taste it to do that."

I rolled my eyes at him, but ate a little slower this time around. I'd always been a quick eater, I just liked food too much. Seth's cooking was so damn good, I didn't know how to do anything but scarf it down. I'd never understand how Theo ate one noodle at a time, they took *forever* to eat, and often didn't finish their food. I still finished my second plate before they were even done with their first.

Being stuffed from scarfing down two plates of food, I leaned against Theo as they took their final bites. Seth, who ate at a pretty normal pace, finished before Theo as well. He started picking up the dishes and I gathered up mine to help clean. I liked doing dishes, it put me in a kind of meditative state. So, I grabbed the pots off the stove after Seth emptied the leftovers into a Tupperware container and set to scrubbing.

Seth went to sit down in front of the television, and I didn't realize Theo was in the kitchen until they wrapped their arms around my stomach as I finished cleaning the final plate. I dried my hands on a dish towel and then turned around, lightly kissing them on the lips. I felt them smile beneath my kiss and then we were moving—up the stairs and into their bedroom. They shut the door behind us and turned around to kiss me deeper as I backed up to their bed.

My hands moved up their back, then to their collar as they went to work slowly helping them unbutton their shirt. They'd been wearing a flannel that was easily tossed to the floor after the final button was undone. I lifted my arms as they pulled my t-shirt over my head, revealing a lacy black bra. Next, I pulled their tank top over their head and paused for a second to look at their face. A grin danced across their lips—no signs of the distress that could rise up in them quickly in these types of situations. They seemed fine so far, so I smiled and pulled them down on top of me on the bed. Their hands ran up my body, sending tingling sensations into my skin each place where they made contact. My back, my shoulders, my neck. Their hands paused on my face, and they leaned down to kiss me again.

I drew in a deep breath as my hands wandered their body, their muscular build firm to the touch. Intertwining my fingers in their hair, I pulled them closer still and kissed their neck. There was a slight flinch to them—a stiffness that hadn't been there a minute ago.

"Are you okay?" I whispered, my lips close to their ear.

"Y-yeah. I'm… no. I need a second." They pulled away from me, sitting up on the bed and putting their hands over their face.

I sat up and rested one of my hands on their lower back, leaning in close, wishing for more. This was the farthest we'd ever gotten, a step in the right direction, but they always froze at some point. Something always held them back. I wished so desperately that I could take that pain away, make whatever horrible experience they had vanish, but I couldn't. All I could do was be patient with them and not pressure them for more, no matter how badly I wanted it.

They took a few deep breaths before dropping their hands in their lap, then looked up at me with tears in their eyes. "I'm sorry I keep doing this. I wish I could do better."

"You're not doing anything wrong, it's okay. Is there anything we can do to make this easier?"

"I don't know, it feels so random when the panic starts. I really want to make you feel good. I feel like such a tease."

"You're not a tease." I brushed a stray lock of hair up out of their face and kissed them on the cheek where a tear rolled down.

"It feels so good, until suddenly it doesn't." They wiped the tears from their face and took another deep breath before looking at me.

Tracing my arm with their hand, they lifted my wrist and kissed the back of my hand. I giggled at that. They were like a knight greeting their queen. Then their hands traveled to my waist, and they moved me onto their lap.

Resting their forehead against mine, they whispered, "I want to try again."

I buried my face in their neck, letting their hands wander down my back and unhook my bra. The air in the room felt cold against my skin, but Theo was so warm. I slid my arms out of my bra straps and then wrapped them around Theo's back, inching as close as I could possibly be with them. My breath caught as their hands ran down my soft stomach to my jeans, where they undid the button and zipper.

"Is this okay?" they asked.

"Yes."

CHAPTER TWO

I awoke first the next day, panicking for a second that I'd forgotten to set an alarm until I checked my phone and realized it was Saturday. Placing my phone back on the shelf lining the bed, I rolled over and wrapped my arms around Theo, burying my face in the crook of their neck and taking in their scent. They stirred, placing their hands on my arms as a smile crept across their face. I closed my eyes, almost falling back asleep when a grumble rose up in Theo's throat.

"What?" I asked.

"I have to pee. But this is so nice, I don't wanna get up."

I snickered at them and pulled my arms away, getting up so that they could go to the bathroom.

"No… come back…"

Rolling my eyes, I smacked them lightly with a pillow. "Go pee."

"Ugh." They rolled over and then pushed themself up on their hands before stumbling out of bed. Their meds made them so groggy in the mornings sometimes I was afraid that they'd fall, but they always managed to catch themself on the walls or chair in their room. I heard the bathroom door shut and then flopped back on the bed, picking up my phone again. Texts from my mother, insisting I come home by 3:00 PM in order to watch my sister again. It was 10:30 AM, so I at least had a bit of time before worrying about that.

Theo stumbled back in the room a few minutes later, going to their dresser and pulling on a pair of joggers over their boxers. "The house smells like French toast."

"Fuck yeah!" Nothing could get me out of bed faster. I threw on one of Theo's old oversized hoodies and a pair of leggings before rushing down the stairs to see Seth in the kitchen.

"I already made you some." He laughed, gesturing towards a plate on the counter.

I sat down eagerly, before Theo even made their way down the stairs, and started pouring syrup over three squares of French toast. Seth made it with cinnamon and vanilla, it was always so sweet. The bread was light and fluffy, practically melting in my mouth. Theo sat down next to me, and Seth set a plate in front of them before sitting down across from us with his own plate.

I glanced around for a minute, noticing the lack of a fourth plate before asking, "Monica's not coming home this morning?"

"She's already here, went to sleep. Long shift last night." Seth replied.

"Oh, okay."

Monica was like a second, much more agreeable mom to me. I enjoyed the conversations we had at times and could go to her with things I couldn't count on my own mother for. She sometimes didn't understand everything, but she did her best and never spoke out of anger with any of us kids. With her, I didn't feel like I had to uphold an impossible standard to gain favor. I could just be me and she'd still love me like her own daughter.

"She's been working a lot lately, hasn't she?"

Seth shrugged, "I think they're short at the hospital. She's too nice to say no."

Theo nodded in agreement while they cut into their toast.

Monica had made an effort to be more available since Theo's hospital stay some months ago. Now that Theo was seemingly doing better I guess she felt more obligated to make up for lost time at work. She'd still come home at the drop of a hat, get someone to cover her shift or something if it was really needed, but she definitely hadn't been home as often in the last couple weeks.

I polished off my toast and set the plate in the sink before sitting down next to Theo again, who still had half a plate of food in front of them.

They glanced over at me before chuckling, "How bad do you want to steal food off my plate right now?"

I'd definitely been thinking about it. "Shut up," I rebutted.

They laughed, sliding their plate over to me with one remaining slice of untouched toast on it. Handing me their fork, they brushed my hair back over my shoulder.

"Is there anything you want to do today?"

"Can we just chill? I don't feel like doing anything, I'm so tired from everything at home and school."

"Sure," they said, almost eagerly.

Theo got up while I was still eating and went into the living room. I turned to watch them flip up the couch cushions and put the back ones on the now bare seat. It created the perfect structure for the sheet that they left the room to grab and returned with a minute later. They laid the sheet over the top, creating a little fort canopy and crawled inside. Hidden in the shade, their hand emerged for the remote and they searched through some shows before landing on our favorite feel-good movie.

"Don't start it without me!" I wolfed down the rest of the toast and then went to the living room, finding Theo stretched out on the couch underneath the fort they'd made with the grin of a proud five-year-old. I crawled in with them and nestled against their chest while they hit play on the movie.

———————

Theo walked me back to my house at 2:45, giving us enough time to stop in front of my door and say goodbye without my mom growing suspicious. We stopped next to the doorframe, careful to avoid sight lines from the windows, and I stole a kiss.

The door opened. I'd regret that.

"I thought I heard something out—Alexandra Anne Kensington!"

My mom froze. We pulled away the instant we'd heard her coming, but weren't fast enough. Theo looked between my mom and I with a panic, and my heart felt like it was going to beat out of my chest.

"Absolutely not!" My mom came out the door and shoved Theo. They took a step back—I was afraid she'd trigger them and they'd react, but they kept their eyes fixed on me.

"Mom!" I ran towards Theo, but my mom put her arm out between the two of us. I looked at them with such fear, and they tried to reach out for me.

"You are to stay away from my daughter, you understand me, freak?" She shoved them again, harder, and this time their gaze flickered to her for a second as they took another step back. If this kept on, they'd lose their composure at some point. So I let them go.

"Theo, please go, it's okay."

They looked at me with a worry I felt in my heart. "Are you sure?"

"Go!" My mom screamed in their face.

I stayed silent as tears started to roll down my cheeks, but I nodded at them. I wanted them out of this situation before it got dangerous for everyone. My mom couldn't be reasoned with. There would never be a way to talk her down.

Slowly, Theo backed away, then turned to leave. They kept stealing glances back at me to make sure I was okay, and I tried to reassure them with my facial expressions. Something told me I wasn't very convincing as my mom whirled on me and grabbed me firmly by the wrist, dragging me inside. She slammed the door behind us and then turned on me, tears brimming in her own eyes.

"Tell me you were not just kissing that girl!"

"Mom, I—"

"Tell me!"

"I love them." I whispered, my whole body shaking with an emotion I couldn't pinpoint. Fear? Anger? Frustration? Everything.

That was all erased with the sharp sting of a slap across my face.

"You do not! You don't ever do that!"

She grabbed me again, and this time I resisted. She jerked my arm forward, causing me to almost trip and fall as she dragged me into the bathroom.

"Take your shirt off."

"What?"

"Take. Your. Shirt. Off."

All the emotions were replaced with pure fear as she pushed me down to the ground in front of the sink. I started crying as I slowly lifted my shirt over my head and curled into a ball, back turned to my mother. I heard a jangling and then there was a pause.

"This is for your own good. You'll never get to heaven with

those impure thoughts."

I almost turned around when the snap of a belt and a searing pain radiated across my back. A yelp escaped me as she hit me again, and again, and again. It felt like forever, I lost count of how many times she hit me. I just stayed curled up, my hands over the back of my head, tears trailing down my cheeks. Each lash sent a new pain searing across my back and compounded on the others. Eventually, she stopped, and though I didn't turn around, I could hear her crying.

"What did I do to deserve a heathen as a daughter?" Her voice was small, weary.

I didn't answer. Everything was shaking. It felt like I couldn't breathe.

"We're going to have a talk when I get home. Give me your phone. I don't want you contacting that girl."

Without looking up at her, I slowly pulled my phone out of my pocket and handed it over.

"Clean yourself up and watch your sister."

With that, she exited the room. I didn't move until I heard the front door open and then slam shut. That's when the sobs came. I pulled my shirt over my raw skin and didn't try to stifle the sound of my crying while I did it. Leah wouldn't hear me anyway. Sitting in the bathroom for what seemed like an eternity, I cried and shook. My mother hated me. This place wasn't safe for me. I couldn't stay here any longer.

Eventually, I peeled myself from the floor and stood up in front of the mirror. My face was bright red, my eyes puffy and swollen from crying. I turned on the water and splashed it on my face, my hands still shaking and nearly causing me to drop the washcloth I picked up to dry my face. I still looked like crap, but it was the best that I was going to get under the circumstances. Taking a few deep breaths, I opened the bathroom door to find Leah on the other side of it.

"What happened? Mom seemed mad. Are you okay?"

Her innocent concern broke me, I started crying again. It didn't take much, I was barely put together in the first place. Leah wrapped her arms around me in a hug as I knelt down to her level. I flinched, the pressure reinviting the searing pain in my back. She meant only the best, but god did it hurt. Nevertheless, I hugged her back. I didn't want her to know what our mother had done. I didn't want that fear in her. I had to stay strong for her. Leah pulled back after a minute and wiped the tears from my face.

"Did she find out about Theo?"

I sighed. She was too smart for her own good. I nodded, and watched as the fear overtook her expression. This wasn't fair, she should never know that fear. It was all because of me, she was the perfect daughter mom had always wanted. I was the one to be discarded.

"It's okay," I signed, "I'm going to make it okay."

I got up and went into my room, where I dug through my closet to pull out a suitcase and then put both it and my backpack on my bed. I had to leave. For everyone's sake. It wasn't safe for me here, and if Leah had to witness what mom did to me it wouldn't be safe for her either. I had to protect her from this hatred, she couldn't be a witness to it. It would scar her in a way that was too late for me to avoid, I would do anything to keep her from feeling what I felt now.

I went through my dresser and closet, pulling out my favorite changes of clothes. I couldn't take everything, so I packed what I liked first. Taking a few books, I also packed a photo album filled with pictures of me and my sister. Once the suitcase was stuffed, I moved on to my backpack and filled it with essentials – toothbrush, hair products, makeup. Leah saw me on my final trip from the bathroom and stood in my doorway as I zipped my backpack.

"You can't leave!" Her signing was frantic, as close to yelling as she would ever get.

"I'm not gonna leave you alone, I'm going to wait until mom gets home and leave after she's asleep."

"I don't want you to leave at all!"

I knelt down in front of her and cupped her face in my hands. "I love you. This is what's best for both of us. I promise I'll try and come see you."

Now she was the one crying. She wrapped her arms around me again and I hugged her back, ignoring the pain this time. I squeezed her tight. I didn't want to leave her. I had no choice. This fucking sucked, but it was all I could do. If I stayed, this house would become a violent place for her, like it already was for me.

"You can't tell mom I'm leaving, okay? Promise."

Slowly, she nodded, the tears coming down from her eyes even faster. I pulled her back in, holding her as she cried. I wished I could just take her with me, get us both out of here. She'd be safe here. Mom would never raise a hand to her. At least, I didn't think so. She had so much more patience for Leah. She never reacted to her the way she treated me. I was thankful for that. I wouldn't have to worry about her getting hurt. Things would probably be better with me gone, she'd have even more time for Leah and less pent-up frustration over her throwaway daughter.

I hid my suitcase and backpack in my closet, then took Leah into the living room where she curled up in my lap as we watched television until bedtime. Then, I took her into her room and tucked her in when she grabbed my arm before I could turn to leave the room.

"I love you, sissy." Her eyes were big and brimming with tears again. Damn, why did this have to be so hard?

I kissed her on the forehead. "I love you too. Forever and always."

She let go of my arm, and I wiped the tears from her face and gave her one last kiss before closing the door behind me. I went into my room, set my shoes by the door and crawled into bed still in my clothes. I'd pretend to be asleep to avoid whatever "talk" mom had in store for me, and once it was safe I'd sneak out the front door.

After a while of tossing and turning, trying to lie in a way that didn't hurt, I heard the front door open and then close softly. I lay still and closed my eyes and listened to the sound of my mother's footsteps. They paused in front of my door, where there was a squeak of the knob turning and the creak of the hinges. After a minute, the door closed again and the footsteps made their way down the hallway until my mom's bedroom door opened and then shut.

I opened my eyes but waited what must've been another twenty minutes before pulling myself out of bed. Grabbing my suitcase and backpack, I struggled to stay quiet as the pain of putting the backpack on shot all across my back. My eyes watered from the pain, but I managed to keep the squeal that tried to escape inside. Picking up the suitcase so as to not let it make noise against the floor, I slowly opened my door. The hallway was dark, save for a small sliver of light coming from under my mom's door that flashed every so often. She had the television on. I could hear it softly from my room. Hopefully that would mask the sound of me leaving.

Holding my breath, I departed from my room and tiptoed on the shag carpet towards the front door. I was carrying my shoes, afraid they'd squeak as soon as I hit the hard wood of the entryway.

Instead, I held my breath as each creak of the wood made me glance back at my mom's bedroom door. Finally, I was at the front door. I set down my suitcase as lightly as possible and then turned the lock on the front door, glancing behind me one final time. I picked up my suitcase again and then I was gone, out the door. I slipped my shoes on while standing on the welcome mat outside, and then took off down the street.

The backpack ground against my back in a way that forced tears out of my eyes, but I didn't care. I just had to get to Theo's. They'd know what to do. I'd be safe there. My pent-up emotions I'd been holding together all night started to overtake me as I walked the empty city street. I kept my head down, avoiding any contact with passersby, at this hour interactions would lead to nothing good. Thankfully it was just a short walk to Theo's—I wasn't sure if they'd even be awake, and I didn't have my phone to text them to let them know I was coming.

As I approached the door, I took a deep breath as tears rolled down my cheeks and then knocked as loudly as possible, praying that someone would answer.

CHAPTER THREE

"Oh, sweetheart, what's wrong?!" Monica's voice prompted more tears as she opened the door and rushed me inside, not even questioning why I'd brought a suitcase. I dropped it on the floor and leaned into her as she wrapped her arms around me, working the backpack off my shoulders. This time I couldn't contain the yelp, and she pulled away, turning me around and dropping the bag.

"There's blood on your shirt."

I grabbed the bottom of my shirt and pulled it down as Monica's fingertips brushed the hem in an instinct to lift it up and assess the damage. She placed a hand calmly, but firmly, on my shoulder.

"Sweetie, let me see."

I let go. She was a doctor, after all, and I had no idea what my back looked like. I just knew it hurt so fucking bad. She lifted the back of my shirt up to my neck and tried to hide the gasp she let out. She lightly touched some places on my back, her cold hands soothing the burn that I felt.

"Who did this?"

"My… my mom." I couldn't stop it, I started sobbing right there in the middle of the kitchen, my whole body shaking.

"Well, that explains the bags. Let me get Theo." She ran her hand gently along my arm after pulling my shirt back down.

She rushed up the stairs and came back down a minute later, a very sleepy looking Theo following behind her. They blinked at the light, but once they saw me it was like they'd had cold water splashed in their face. They ran over to me, gently placing their hands on my arms.

"What did she do?"

I pointed to my back, and felt them freeze when they saw the blood on my shirt.

"I never should've left you." Their tone filled with remorse.

"It's… it's not your fault. I told you to go."

"Theo, why don't you take her up to the bathroom and get her cleaned up? I'll put her bags in the guest room down here. You'll stay here tonight, Alex."

Theo silently guided me up the stairs and into the bathroom. They ran the bathtub with warm water and put in the bubble bath that they knew I loved. I was still crying. I didn't know if I would ever stop. Theo wasn't talking—to be fair, they didn't normally talk much, but this was a different kind of silence. This was stiff. They were holding something back. It made me anxious, not knowing what they were thinking. Once the bathtub was half full, they stopped the tap and then turned to me, glancing briefly at my face before focusing on my clothes. It felt like they were avoiding eye contact as they undid my belt and slid my pants down. They carefully lifted my shirt over my head, trying not to aggravate the welts. I regained my composure enough to take my bra off myself, then slid out of my underwear and into the bath.

I was confused when Theo turned around—then they started undressing as well. The last thing to go was their binder, and then they slid into the bath just behind me and wrapped their arms around my shoulders. Their hands weren't wet yet but I felt a dampness—they were crying.

Then, so quietly I almost missed it, "I never wanted you to know what this felt like."

I lost my composure again at that. They leaned back, picking up a washcloth, glancing at my back, and then putting it back down, seemingly thinking better of it. Instead, they lathered some soap between their hands and with the lightest touch started washing each mark on my back. I winced at the burning sensation that the soap prompted, but it was over soon enough. After they were done, I curled up into Theo's arms and rested my head on their chest. I traced my fingers along their collarbone for a minute, staring at the contrast between their brown olive-toned skin and my ghostly white hands that looked even paler in the harsh bathroom light.

"Has she ever hurt you before?" Theo's question broke my concentration and I glanced up at their face before answering.

"She hit me once, the day my dad left. I never told anyone. It was nothing like this."

They didn't miss a beat. "Did she hit you with a belt?"

"How could you tell?"

"My bio father used to hit me with a belt, left the same kind of marks. One time it got infected and I got so sick he had to take me to the hospital. That's how I got taken away."

Suddenly, I felt incredibly weak for how much I'd cried over this in comparison with Theo's history. This was nothing. "I feel silly for how upset I am over this. You've had so much worse."

Theo brushed away a lock of hair that had fallen in my face.

"Don't try and compare suffering, that doesn't help anyone. Your pain is just as valid. You're not silly for being upset that your mother hurt you."

They kissed me on the forehead, resting their palm against my temple and stroking my hair. I felt so safe here with them, as if in a cocoon, on another planet away from all the pain and fear. We stayed like that until the water turned cold and we both became shivering messes covered in goosebumps. We finally relented and got out, only to realize we hadn't brought clothes in with us.

Theo wrapped up in a towel and made an escape to their room while I waited for them in the bathroom. After a few minutes, I heard footsteps down the stairs, and then back up. They came back in, fully dressed in an oversized hoodie and joggers, and handed me a small stack of clothing that I quickly changed into. Leggings and my favorite hoodie of Theo's. Clothes that felt warm against my frigid skin, hoodie loose enough that it didn't aggravate my back. We cleaned up and then both went into Theo's room where we cuddled together in their bed. They wrapped me in so many blankets, then took me in their arms, holding me close in the dark room we'd forgotten to turn a light on in.

There was a knock on the door, and Theo mustered a "Come in." It was Monica, who turned on the desk light and then pulled up Theo's rolling chair.

"Alex, you can stay here as long as you need, but we need to figure out what to do about this. What your mother did is abuse."

My face got hot, and I tried to force back the tears that appeared in my eyes. I'd cried enough tonight. "I don't want to report anything. I don't want to risk getting Leah taken away. She'd never hurt her like this. That's her home, I can't just take that away from her."

"What makes you think she won't do this to Leah? If she's capable of doing this to one of her children—"

"She won't." I interrupted, "She's always loved Leah more. She's barely tolerated me for a long time, we never got along. She only did this because she found out that Theo and I are together."

"She did this because she thinks you're gay?"

I sighed. "Yes."

Monica shook her head and stood up, placing a hand gently on my shoulder. "Let me think on this. You're always welcome here, okay?"

Nodding, I watched Monica leave and close the door behind her. I buried myself in Theo's arms, and they held me tight. I was safe here. At least I'd always have a safe place.

———

I was slow to get up the next morning. I awoke before Theo, still encased in my cocoon of blankets. Wriggling my way out of them, I did my best to not wake Theo. Eventually, I freed myself from the pile and took in a deep, exasperated breath. That was a lot more effort than I'd planned on expending as soon as I'd woken up.

My mom would probably just now be realizing that I was gone. Truth be told, I wasn't sure what her reaction would be. Relief? Anger? Surprise? Maybe all three, maybe even more. Her favorite daughter was still there, so I'm sure she wouldn't miss a beat in whisking her off to church this sleepy Sunday morning. Maybe she'd ask the church to pray for me. I rolled my eyes at the thought. I didn't need prayer, I needed a mother whose love wasn't conditional. Everyone would buy her sob story, no questions asked. Her daughter had strayed from the path of God, lured by a sexual deviant, probably worshipping the devil in her spare time. At least, that sounded like a story she'd tell. She'd make herself the victim in this somehow. Not the mother that assaulted her daughter because she'd kissed the person she loved.

A light touch on my hip broke my train of thought, startled me and caused me to jerk my head around to see that Theo had woken up. As they looked at me through squinted eyes, I tried to calm my racing heart. Why was I so jumpy? I knew I was safe here.

"You're shaking, what's wrong?" Theo asked, their speech slightly slurred with sleep.

I hadn't noticed, I'd been so lost in my thoughts about my mother. I took a deep breath and tried to steady myself, leaning back into Theo's arms.

"I'm just thinking about my mom."

"Fuck her." They said abruptly, "She doesn't deserve you."

I nestled my head into the crook of Theo's neck, taking in their scent and closing my eyes. They rested their arms around me, careful to avoid my back. They brushed my hair away from my face as I looked up into their golden eyes. One trait I'd always found striking, so much so that my heart would skip a beat sometimes when I'd look at them. Tracing their face with my fingertips, I caught their chin and guided it towards my mouth for a kiss. Their lips were so soft, their touch always so gentle.

I lost myself in the moment, until I heard a knock on the door and shot upwards with a squeal, my heart begging for my nerves to stop jolting it, leaving me feeling like I'd run a marathon. Theo sat up almost as quickly, and then let out a deep sigh of relief. I'd likely scared them with my reaction. Without even addressing the door, they turned to me and placed their hands on my shoulders.

"It's okay, it's safe here. No one's going to hurt you." They gently turned my head towards them, my gaze still fixed on the door before glancing to them for a brief second. Another knock meant my eyes darted right back. I knew it would either be Seth or Monica at the door, yet my brain was sending signals as if it were my mother behind it. Theo's hands lingered on my shoulders for a minute as they got up from the bed to answer the door.

It was Seth. "Hey, I made breakfast if either of you want some, I'm about to bounce so should I put it away or do you have it?"

"We got it." Theo nodded at him, "Thank you."

Seth nodded back and then left the doorway. Theo shut the door and turned around, sitting on the bed next to me.

"See? It's okay. Hey, look at me." They guided my chin so that my eyes locked with theirs. "No one's going to hurt you here."

I blinked hard and tried to center myself, I'd never felt panic so intense. Is this what an anxiety attack felt like? God, I didn't envy Theo at all. This was awful. I was shaking and breathing so erratically, I thought I might pass out.

Theo wrapped their arms around my back, pulling me into their chest. They squeezed me tight. The pressure felt so good to help calm my body, and I clung to them while trying to slow my breathing.

"I don't know what's wrong with me, why I'm like this all of the sudden." I whispered, still holding tight to them.

"It's a trauma response, Al, my therapist talks about them all the time. You react to situations like they're dire because they were once. It takes a lot of work to make them calm down. What your mom did was traumatizing."

"So… so you feel like this all the time?"

"A lot of the time, yeah."

I lifted my head to meet their eyes and ran my hand down their face. "I'm so sorry."

"Like I said, I never wanted you to know what this felt like."
They ran a hand down my arm. "C'mon, let's go get breakfast."

I got up and followed them down the stairs, met with the scent of eggs, bacon, and toast with cheese. Breakfast sandwiches– Theo's favorite. They eagerly scooped up the runniest looking egg with a spatula and put it on the bread with some bacon and started chowing down. I made mine in a similar fashion, except choosing the least runny egg and a couple extra crispy pieces of bacon. We didn't even bother to sit down and ate standing by the sink. Once we were finished, Theo put away the leftovers and I did the dishes. Afterwards, we curled up in the little couch fort that was still standing and turned on the television.

Monica came home about a half hour later, sighing as she hung her keys by the door and took off her shoes. Theo and I poked our heads out of the fort to say hello. It must've been a rough shift, she looked disheveled and exhausted. I could've sworn there was some blood on the hem of her scrubs. She gave us a weak smile and pulled some leftovers out of the fridge to stick them in the microwave.

A knock on the door interrupted her as she was about to take a bite of her sandwich, and she muttered as she went to open the door and was met with angry demands.

"Where is she?!" My mother shouted in Monica's face, taking a step inside.

Monica didn't miss a beat. "Where you can't hurt her."

I peered through the crack in the couch cushions to see her roll her eyes at Monica, but stayed hidden in the fort. All the hairs on my arms were standing up, I started shaking involuntarily and put a hand over my mouth to keep quiet.

"That's ridiculous. Is that what you call disciplining a child now? Hurting them? No wonder yours turned out as freaks. No discipline, no father to keep them in line."

"You need to leave." Monica's tone was flat, she didn't even entertain my mother's hurtful accusations.

"Not until I get my daughter. I'm taking her somewhere where they'll help her with her sick delusions. They'll sort her out."

Monica's voice raised a pitch. "You're talking about a conversion camp. You know those places are illegal? They do nothing but traumatize children who just need acceptance."

"I cannot accept a heathen. They will bring her back to God."

"Get out of my house."

"Alexandra? Come out now and things will be easier for you."

Theo placed a hand on my shoulder, indicating that I should stay where I was. They got up from the couch and placed themself behind Monica, their expression angry and much less patient than her.

"You never should've hit her." They growled.

"You never should've dragged her into sin, you freak!"

Theo took a step forward, but Monica put her arm out to stop them. "Theo, let me handle this."

"If you don't give me my daughter, I'll get the police involved."

"Do it and I'll tell them exactly what you did to her and where you are planning to send her. I'll show them the marks on her back and how she came to me in tears after you beat her." Monica took a step closer to my mother, barely an inch from her face and calmly said, "Now I'll tell you for the last time, get out of my house."

My mother stood there in stunned silence with her mouth hanging open for a minute before huffing and walking away. Monica closed and locked the door behind her. Theo came back over to me, and Monica also came over and sat on the coffee table in front of me. I was shaking harder than I'd like to admit, and tears were brimming in my eyes. Theo wrapped me in their arms and Monica placed a hand on my knee.

"I won't let her take you to a place like that, okay? I promise to keep you safe here." Monica's tone had softened considerably now that she was addressing me.

Tears ran down my cheeks. I'd heard stories of conversion camps – places where parents sent queer kids to "fix" them. They used scripture as their excuse for inhumane treatment of kids, going as far as beating and drugging them until they started to deny that they were queer. I'd never survive a place like that.

I got up and hugged Monica, and she embraced me back, careful to avoid the sore spots on my back.

"Please don't let her take me." I whispered, feeling so helpless.

"Never." Monica cooed.

CHAPTER FOUR

The police never called or came by the house, so I assumed that Monica's threats of telling the truth had scared my mother off. This meant that my mother knew what she did was wrong in the eyes of the law. I didn't understand how you could know that and still be so convinced that you were right or were doing the right thing. I couldn't imagine treating my own child the way she had treated me.

I was still anxious about her showing up at school as we walked in on Monday morning. For once, the bullies weren't my concern. Theo stayed close by me, able to sense my unease. Our first class was together thankfully, so they could stay by my side.

I couldn't focus on anything the teacher was saying, I knew it was science and that we were preparing for a lab, but everything felt so distant, so surreal. It was like I wasn't really in my body, I was floating above everything and listening through a thick glass pane that distorted my view and hearing. Theo kept stealing glances at me, and I barely noticed. I couldn't reassure them that I was okay. I wasn't okay. At one point, everyone got up and partnered with each other, but I hadn't heard why. Theo walked over to me and gently placed a hand on mine.

"Alex?" Their voice was distant, muffled.

I didn't respond, it felt like my body and brain were moving through molasses.

They moved their hand to my shoulder and squeezed slightly. The pressure brought me back to reality a little, but everything still felt surreal. I looked up at them slowly, my eyes unfocused.

They let me go and approached the teacher as I floated away again, staring in their general direction but unable to pick one object to focus on. The teacher's head turned in my direction and then seemed to move in a nod as Theo turned and made their way back to me. They placed a hand on my shoulder again and leaned in.

"I'm taking you to the nurse."

My body moved without me thinking. Theo guided me up and took my hand to lead me out of the classroom. My legs felt like lead, and Theo slowed down as I struggled to keep up with them. The surroundings seemed to pass quickly while I was moving at a snail's pace. We staggered by a group of kids my brain refused to recognize, but I was reminded too quickly as one of them slapped me on the back.

I shrieked. The pain radiated across my raw skin and was enough to break me. Tears started streaming down my face and I fell to the ground, my legs refusing to support me any longer. Laughter echoed around me as I sobbed, unable to regain any composure, not having the energy to try. It was as if I were alone in the center of a stage with a spotlight blaring in my eyes with an audience full of hecklers watching. Unable to see the threat, but knowing all too well that it was there.

After what felt like an eternity, a light touch on my shoulders startled me, and I jerked away before realizing that it was Theo.

The bullies were gone, but I hadn't been aware of what was going on, so I had no idea what Theo had done to get them to leave. I hoped it wasn't anything too drastic that they'd regret later. I hadn't been there to keep the peace. Gently, they lifted me to my feet, and we resumed our walk to the nurse.

Once we arrived in the nurse's office, Theo helped me into a chair and walked up to the nurse's desk. The short-haired brunette with hazel eyes looked up at them through her thick-rimmed glasses and gave a reassuring smile.

"Hey Theo, do you need your medication?"

"No… uh, maybe. But that's not why I'm here." They gestured towards me, and the nurse peered over the desk.

I was still crying, albeit the sobs were no longer taking over my body. Shaking, I tried to focus on the nurse as she came out from behind her desk and kneeled in front of me.

"Alex, what's wrong? Do I need to call your mother?"

My attention snapped onto that final word. "No!" I shouted, then tried to reel myself in. "I mean, no. Please don't call my mom."

I couldn't tell the nurse what happened. She was a mandated reporter. She'd have to call child protective services over the welts on my back, and who knows what hell that would bring for Leah, for me. I had a safe place to go, but legalities would get in the way of that, and I'd be forced into a group home or something similar. I knew enough about the system from what Theo and Seth had told me about their experiences. Theo had been ripped from a good home because the system had decided they were no longer equipped to handle them. Monica was a single mother with two adopted children, no way would a social worker be eager to let me stay there. No, no one at school could find out.

"She didn't look good, I think she just needs a little break."

Theo kept things vague as well, I'm sure they had the same thought process that I did.

The nurse glanced between the two of us, then gestured to the couch on the opposite side of her office. "Why don't you lie down? I'll get you some water."

Theo guided me over to the couch to have me lie down, then knelt in front of me to stroke my hair and brush it out of my face. The nurse returned a minute later with a cup of water that I took. Things were gradually starting to come into focus, I felt a little more like I was actually inside my body. I sat up to sip the water, placing my feet firmly on the ground and trying to focus on my surroundings. I'd seen Theo do it a hundred times before, wiggle their toes against the floor in their shoes and pick something to focus on in the room, then move on to the next thing once they'd analyzed the first.

The nurse stood in front of us, trying to assess the situation. I'd never actually been in this office for myself before. She knew this was unusual. I'd helped Theo here countless times between their fights and panic attacks, but I'd never been here for me.

Theo saw the intensity with which the nurse was trying to grasp what was going on. They saw the bigger picture, then quickly glanced between her and myself.

"You know, I think I do need my meds," they said with a weak smile.

The nurse nodded and retreated behind her desk to pull out a pill bottle and another cup of water, then handed them to Theo. They took a pill out of the container and swallowed with a few gulps of water before the nurse took the bottle back and then pulled her rolling chair over to the couch.

"Alex, what happened? I've never seen you like this."

"I uh… I…" Shit. What was I supposed to say? I couldn't think of any explanation that wouldn't give me away.

"The usual group of scumbags were out in the hallway. They got a hit in before I could stop them." Theo jumped in, "She's never gotten hit before, I usually block for her."

Well, half of that was true. I'd gotten hit before, plenty of times. In the halls when Theo wasn't around, I was a much easier target. I never told them, I knew they'd just be angry and upset that they weren't able to protect me every time. Still, it was a much better explanation than anything I could come up with.

The nurse nodded slowly. I wasn't sure if she was buying it, but she didn't pry any further. "How are you feeling now, Alex?"

I took in a deep breath. "A little better, thanks."

She gave me a weak smile and nodded. "Take a couple more minutes if you need, this period's almost over. I'll write you a note and you two can go back for next period."

"Okay," I managed.

Theo sat down next to me on the couch, and I leaned into them, taking in their scent. They always said that smell was what brought them back to reality the quickest. They would use a specific lotion sometimes, so I took in the safest scent I knew—theirs. Things were a lot clearer now. I was in school. In the nurse's office. Theo had their arm around my shoulders. There was a cup of water in my hands. The fluorescent lighting was as headache-inducing as ever. And I was okay.

————

The next class was a blur again—Theo dropped me off to make sure I made it okay, but they had a different class so we had to split up. I spent most of this math class trying to focus on my surroundings and not lose touch with reality again. I had so much more understanding for how Theo's day-to-day was, just from this one morning, suddenly all of their behaviors made so much more sense to me. I'd want to get drunk or high if I felt like this all the time too, and I was sure this wasn't all of what they had to deal with. This was just anxiety. Really intense anxiety, but anxiety all the same. I didn't have the dreams, the memories, the flashbacks, the anger that they carried. That all seemed like too much.

Even just this was too much.

My day came more into focus as my plastic tray clattered on the table when I sat down in the cafeteria across from Theo. Jeremy was already there. The two were making plans to go skateboarding after school. I glanced quickly between them before focusing on my tray. The sudden movement of Theo's hand on mine made me jump, and I caught the back end of what they were saying.

"...Unless you need me to stay home?"

I gave a forced smile and shook my head, not wanting to keep them. Skateboarding was their release. They always seemed so clear-headed afterwards. I didn't want to take that away from them. Barely noticing as Jeremy looked me up and down, I remained silent.

"How are you doing?" Theo prodded, not accepting my wordless answer.

"I'm… I'm a little better. I think. It's hard to focus on things still."

"Why don't you come with us? I know you're not a huge fan of the skate park, but what if I started teaching you some things? You don't notice the people as much when you're boarding."

I laughed at that. "I'd fall on my ass in two seconds."

"That's part of the fun! Plus, when you get it, it feels so good. C'mon, why don't we try?"

Jeremy chimed in, "Yeah, you should try! I'll lend you my helmet since Theo's reckless and doesn't wear one."

I couldn't stop the grin that made its way across my face. Theo had never offered to teach me before. I'd never thought to ask. "Okay, sure."

"What's up with you, anyway? You seem… weird." Jeremy elbowed my arm to get my attention as I'd started pushing my food around on my tray again without realizing it.

"I'm… I don't…" I sighed, dropping my fork and rubbing my temples lightly with my fingertips.

Theo lowered their voice, "He gets it Al, you know that. It's okay."

I wasn't close with Jeremy like Theo was. There had been some tension between me and Jeremy for the longest time. We just didn't hit it off like Theo and Jeremy did. We were okay now, we came together for Theo's sake and honestly the more time I spent with him the more I liked him, but I wasn't sure if I was ready to trust him with this yet. I knew he understood from dealing with his own mother. He came to school with fresh bruises constantly. He wouldn't tell anyone unless I asked him to. It was a safe place to let it out. Maybe I'd give him the chance.

But I couldn't look at him while I did it. I stared down at my food and pushed it around some more while mumbling. "My mom, she found out about me and Theo. She hit me with a belt. I've been staying at Theo's house."

Jeremy's dark eyes widened and stole a look at Theo before focusing back on me. "Shit, I'm sorry Alex. That fucking sucks." He put a hand on my shoulder, "We've got you, okay?"

Tears that I couldn't stop brimmed in my eyes. He was so sincere, and I'd never helped at all when it came to his mom. I'd have to be a better friend to him in the future.

The rest of the day floated by. I fought through my brain to try and focus but ultimately it wouldn't have made a difference if I'd skipped school entirely. I had no idea what any of the teachers had said in any of the classes. My brain felt empty, and each interaction just echoed through me like I was in a cavern with people shouting. I wasn't thinking about my mom, I wasn't thinking about *anything*. It felt so strange, and I tried so hard to get my brain to stay present in my body. There was a word for this, I knew it, but I couldn't remember.

Theo held me close on the bus until we both got off at their house. We stopped in briefly while Theo pulled out their board and then began digging through their closet, until finally they pulled out a helmet that was plastered in stickers.

"What is that?" I chuckled, brought into the present by the absurdity of what they were holding in their hands.

"Hey, just because I don't use it doesn't mean I don't have one."

"No," I laughed, "The stickers. They look like a ten-year-old put them on there."

The stickers were pictures of rainbow dogs and unicorns, reminiscent of Lisa Frank artwork.

"That's because I did, that's the last time I used it."

"And you're gonna make me wear it."

"Of course I am, what kind of partner would I be if I didn't protect that precious head of yours?"

I rolled my eyes and took it from their hands as we left their room and walked down the stairs to leave. We met Jeremy shortly after at the skate park. It was still the afternoon, so most of the people there were recreational skaters. Kids with their parents, young teens with their friends.

I was about to make an absolute fool of myself.

Theo placed their board in front of me and tightened the

helmet on my head. I looked at them blankly until they took my hips in their hands.

"First we've gotta just get you used to being on it."

They guided me over to the skateboard, where I hesitantly took a step. The board moved slightly and all of my body weight threw backwards as if I'd slipped on a banana peel. Theo's grip on my hips tightened as they steadied me, stopping me from falling. Hesitantly, I put my second foot up on the board and tried my best to keep my balance. Theo was doing most of the balancing for me, their firm hands keeping me in place. I stole a glance at them swiftly, their concentration so focused on my body and posture that they didn't notice. Their golden eyes were trained downwards at the board and my feet, the wisps of their hair fluttered in the slight spring breeze.

I got distracted looking at them, and my unsteady balance gave out. Throwing my arms forward did little to help, and Theo caught me in their arms as I fell back off the board. They giggled a little at me as I tried to get my feet back underneath myself. It was as if we were caught in the middle of a dance, except far less elegant. Our eyes locked for a second and they gave me a reassuring smile as I got my footing on solid ground and they went to grab the board that had rolled away. They came back and placed the board in front of me for a second time.

"Try again, maybe a little less checking me out this time."

Jeremy laughed from the few paces back where he was standing, and Theo's sly smile held back their laughter as well. I never was a subtle flirt.

Theo placed their hands on my hips again, and this time I did my best to focus on the board, each jerky movement throwing my weight around as I placed my first foot down.

"Don't look at the board either, it'll throw you off. Look where you want to go."

"Oh, okay." I lifted my head to stare at a spot on the pavement a few feet away, then picked up my second foot to place on the board. I was shaky, but this time I was balancing a bit better. Theo waited until I stopped waving my arms around trying to get steady, until I was standing on the board with only a little wobble.

"There you go! Relax into it. Ready to move?"

"How?"

"I'll move you at first, just keep your balance."

They took a few steps sideways, still holding onto my hips, slowly moving me forwards. My weight jerked around at first, but I was eventually able to find my center of balance. And then I was moving, albeit slowly, towards the spot on the pavement I had my eyes trained on. I started laughing, once Theo stopped moving me and looked up at my face.

"Look, you did it!"

With their help, I came to a stop. I was starting to see the appeal, focusing all my concentration on moving to that one spot had taken my mind off of so many things. Accomplishing it felt *so good*.

"Now you try it without me."

"What?" My head snapped back to them in a yelp as I jumped off the board the second their hands were no longer on my hips. The absence of their grasp guiding me made my heart jump, as if I was a little kid suddenly realizing they were alone in the supermarket.

They put their hands on my shoulders and looked up at me, "It's okay, I'll stay close. Try and just balance without me holding you."

I picked up the board and moved it back to our original spot with Theo following, then put one foot up. Theo was just inches from me with their arms out, ready to catch me should I fall. That was enough reassurance for me to take a deep breath and pick my second foot up.

Immediately, the board rolled forward a little and I threw my weight in the opposite direction, causing more forward momentum and completely losing any semblance of stability that I had. Theo reached for me, but I fell away from them, and it was Jeremy that caught my shoulders just before my face collided with the pavement. I put my hands out to catch myself and Jeremy slowly lowered me to the ground. I sat up on the pavement, no worse for wear, but my pride a little hurt.

"Damn."

"It's okay," Theo knelt in front of me, "You have no idea how long it took me to get the hang of it. Getting on is the hardest part. Why don't I hold you this time and I'll let go once you find your center?"

I nodded, getting up and pulling the board back again. Theo's familiar touch graced my hips as I stepped on the board with both feet, a little faster this time. I wobbled, but Theo held me steady. Once the wobbling stopped, Theo's grasp on my hips slowly loosened, until they pulled their hands away completely. I held myself steady for a minute, engaging muscles I didn't even know I had in order to stay upright on the board. After a solid sixty seconds, one of my legs jerked from the tension, but this time I caught myself by putting my foot down on the ground before I fell.

"Nice!" Theo called, holding their hand up for a high five.

I gave it to them, laughing at their eagerness over me standing on a board for a seemingly insignificant amount of time when they could flip the board in the air and still land on it with ease. Unclipping the garish helmet and taking it off my head, I pushed the board back over to Theo.

"Why don't you skate for a while? I think I need a break."

Theo stepped on the tail end of the board and flipped it up into their hand before throwing their other arm around the back of my neck and pulling me down for a kiss that I wasn't expecting. I leaned into it, wrapping my arms around their waist and pulling in their warmth. They pulled away and then brushed a stray lock of hair out of my face.

"What was that for?" My sheepish expression gave away that I wanted more.

"For trying." They beamed, their smile melting my heart.

With that, they tagged Jeremy on the back and dropped their board to the ground before jumping on and speeding towards a ramp. I watched as they closed their eyes, their stance relaxed as they felt the wind on their face. It was as if all the weight fell from their shoulders and for a moment they looked effortless, free.

CHAPTER FIVE

Screams awoke me from a fitful sleep that I'd barely fallen into. I was in the guest room downstairs. I'd been working on homework and must've dozed off somewhere along the way. Pushing the papers to the side, I got up out of the bed as my mind raced through the hundreds of things that could be wrong. Was there an intruder? Was someone hurt? It sounded like it might be Theo, but I'd never heard them scream this way. It was a raw, unbridled scream that exuded pure terror. Opening the door, I peeked my head out to find the house empty, then ran up the stairs—the screams were indeed coming from Theo's room. I threw the door open to see Theo tossing in bed, kicking and flailing as if someone were attacking them.

This must be one of their night terrors. Seth had mentioned them to me before, but I never imagined they'd be so intense. They were on medication to help with them, but I guessed some found their way to the surface regardless. They'd never had one when we slept in the same bed, which was most times when I was over.

I approached the bed and tried to contain their wildly flailing body. "Theo!"

I was answered by more soul-piercing shrieks, the occasional incoherent word being shouted as their face scrunched and grimaced in pain.

Dodging their flailing arms, I tried to wake them again. "T, baby, you're dreaming." Tears brimmed in my eyes—they were in so much pain, I just wanted to stop it.

Suddenly Seth was at my side. He gave me a knowing look and then caught an arm just as it was about to collide with my face. Instinctively, I backed up. Seth knew how to handle this better than I did. He'd done it before. He leaned over them on the bed, pinning Theo down. This seemed to trigger even more intense fighting in the moment, but then Seth rubbed at Theo's breastbone with his knuckles so hard they turned white.

Theo's eyes flew open with a final scream that morphed into words. "Ow, you fucker!" They shot up in bed as Seth released them and they frantically looked around the room.

Seth sighed, "Alex, you can come here now."

I rushed to Theo's side, wrapping my arms around them. They fell into me, clinging to my shoulders. Seth got up, placing a hand on my shoulder and Theo's hand briefly before leaving the room, closing the door behind him.

"Did I hurt you?" Theo's voice was hoarse, but the concern still came through their muffled words with their face buried in my chest.

"No, baby. Seth came in just a minute after I got here." I didn't tell them about the hand that nearly caught my face. They'd just feel terrible.

They pulled away slightly, looking at me with tears in their eyes. "Always let him wake me up, okay? I don't want you to get hurt. I've hurt both him and Mom before. I don't know what I'd do if I hurt you."

"This has never happened when I've been here before, was that a night terror?"

"Yes," they said, breathless. "I don't get them when you sleep with me."

I pulled my legs up onto the bed, positioning myself between Theo and the wall, cradling them in my arms. My hands ran through their hair as they wiped away the tears.

"Do you want your meds? Do they help with this?"

"No, no I'm okay. I never remember them after I wake up. I'll never get up in the morning if I take meds now." They laced their arms into mine and pulled the blanket up over both of us with a sigh.

"That thing, what did he do to wake you up? It seemed like it hurt."

"Mom was the first one to try it, doctors use it to wake up patients sometimes. I guess it's the only thing that really wakes me up when I'm like that. It's Seth's go-to now, I think he just got tired of getting hit, I don't blame him."

"Does it, though? Hurt?"

They pulled their tank top down a bit to reveal a red mark in the middle of their chest, "Like a bitch."

A yawn escaped me a second later, and I started to slouch in the bed.

Theo glanced up at me, "I'm sorry I woke you up, I know you haven't been feeling good."

"No, it's okay. I wasn't sleeping great anyway. I woke up in a pile of homework I was trying to do."

They sat up for a second so that I could settle properly into the bed, then lay back down, arms encircling my waist. I had no idea what time it was, but in the moment I didn't really care. I loved the cuddles Theo gave me, they were so warm and comforting. Nothing felt more like home. Letting out a deep sigh, I drifted off to sleep.

———————

The thing that woke me the next morning wasn't the alarm but Theo's deep grumble of "Fuuuuck" in response to it. They sat up and clutched their stomach, doubling over in pain. Footsteps rang through my head as they quickly got up and ran to the bathroom. I drifted off to sleep for a second before a knock on the wall woke me all over again.

"Alex?" Theo's voice was muffled through the wall.

"Yeah?" I got up and pressed my ear to the wall so that I could hear them better.

"Could you bring me a change of underwear please? Not boxers."

"Okay." Turning away, I dug through the top drawer of their dresser to find a pair of boy shorts style underwear and knocked on the bathroom door.

Theo cracked the door open and took them, closing the door swiftly afterwards.

"Are you okay?"

"Yeah, I just got my fucking period."

I sighed with relief, I was worried that they were sick or something. Going back to the bedroom, I curled back up in bed briefly, hoping to catch five more minutes of sleep. A minute later, Theo came in and sat on the edge of the bed, with their face in their hands. A sniffle came from their direction, and I reached up to rub their back.

"What's wrong?" I kept my voice low.

"I just fucking hate it, it gives me such bad dysphoria. And it hurts."

"Oh, T, I'm sorry." The idea of dysphoria from a period hadn't occurred to me. Now that it did, I felt like kind of an ass for not realizing it. I sat up and wrapped my arms around them.

"I get such bad cramps, it feels like someone's ripping my stomach out. Mom's tried everything for me and nothing seems to help. What do you do for them?"

My face flushed. Embarrassment reaching down to every inch of me. "Um…"

They placed a hand over one of mine, likely feeling how hot I'd gotten. "There's nothing to be embarrassed about, we both get them."

"Actually, I… I've never had one."

They turned suddenly to look back at me, "Serious?"

"Yeah, my mom says that people in my family get it late."

"Al, you're sixteen, how late are we talking?"

"I… I don't know. She never told me. Every time I asked about it she just told me we'd talk about it when I finally got it."

"That sounds a little off. I think you should tell Mom about it."

"What's she gonna do, make it magically appear? I know she's a doctor but even medicine has its limits." I rolled my eyes in fake exasperation.

"No, Al, I'm serious. Something might be wrong."

The worry on their face stopped me in my tracks. I took their chin in my hands and kissed them lightly.

"Okay, I'll talk to Monica."

Theo got up and finished getting dressed, practically doubled over the whole time. I felt so bad, but it was a pain I couldn't kiss away for them. A pain I'd never felt, but I knew it had to be bad in order to knock Theo out like this. I got dressed as well and we both went down to the kitchen to find something to eat. Monica was leaning over the sink with a cup of coffee, Seth nowhere in sight. He must've slept in after being woken up last night. Theo rummaged through the pantry for some cereal while I pulled milk out of the fridge.

"Mom, can I have some ibuprofen? I have cramps." Theo glanced briefly in Monica's direction while pulling some Apple Jacks out of the cupboard.

Monica nodded, running upstairs to grab her keys and coming back down to unlock the cabinet above the sink. With Theo's track record with medications, Monica kept everything prescription and otherwise under lock and key. Theo had a week's worth of medication in their pill organizer upstairs, not enough to cause too much damage if taken all at once. Monica took out a bottle of ibuprofen and tipped three pills into her hand before handing them to Theo.

"Shit, I didn't take my meds." Theo muttered while taking the pills into their hands. They went back up the stairs while shouting behind them, "Alex needs to talk to you about something."

Fuck. I hadn't meant *now.* But now I was stuck in the kitchen holding a carton of milk while Monica turned around to face me with concern in her eyes. The same look she'd given me when I'd showed up at the door with a suitcase and tears in my eyes.

"What's the matter, sweetheart?"

My face flushed red. I was so embarrassed about this, and I didn't even know why. It's not like I could control it. Monica took a step forward and placed a hand gingerly on my shoulder and looking directly into my eyes with her piercing light green irises.

"It's okay, you can tell me."

"I… just… Theo and I were talking and I mentioned I've never had my period. They got worried."

"Never? Not even a little bit of bleeding here and there?"

"No."

"Huh…" She took a step back and placed her hand on her chin like she was thinking.

"My… my mom said that people in my family get it late, so I never really worried about it."

"I mean… it's possible. But it is a little out of the ordinary. I think we should make you an appointment to get checked out. Have you ever been?"

"No, my mom never talked to me about that kind of stuff, I'm not even sure she goes."

"I have a friend who does it, she's very good. Is it all right if I make an appointment with her for you?"

"O-okay."

"I wouldn't worry until we know what's going on, for all we know your mom could've been right. No use getting worked up when we don't even know if there's something to be worked up about."

I hadn't been worried until she said that. Now I nervously twisted a lock of hair between my fingers, setting the milk on the counter. What if there was something wrong, what did that even mean? If I looked it up online, I'd probably end up down a rabbit hole that ended in cancer, so I decided against it, only briefly touching my pocket where I'd normally keep the phone I forgot my mom still had. I'd need a new one, because I sure wasn't getting that one back.

Theo descended the stairs with their backpack in one hand and phone in the other, and I pulled bowls out of the cupboard near the fridge, trying to get my mind off the small crisis my brain had fallen into about all this. I must've been making a face, because Theo dropped their bag on the floor and made their way over to me, wrapping an arm around my waist.

"You okay?" they whispered in my ear.

Shivers ran down my spine that made my hair stand on end in a good way. Taking in a deep breath, I turned around and kissed them with everything I had. I felt them smile beneath my lips until I slowly pulled away, taking in their beautiful grin.

"Yeah, I'm all right." I grabbed a couple spoons and placed them in the bowls on the kitchen island in front of the stools, and Theo set to pouring out some cereal while I grabbed the milk. We devoured our cereal quickly, noticing that time was running short for us to catch the bus. After eating, I grabbed my backpack from the guest room and practically ran into Seth as he hurried to the kitchen and pulled a granola bar from one of the cupboards. He must've really overslept.

A minute later, we were all standing outside as the bus arrived. We piled on, Seth towards the front, Theo and I in our usual seat near the back. On the ride, Theo braided a particularly stubborn strand of my hair together and then tucked it behind my ear. I loved it when they played with my hair. It was so soothing.

Once we got off the bus, we were surprised to find the usual group of bullies was nowhere in sight. A wave of relief washed over me, knowing that I wouldn't have to deal with their bullshit while Theo and I grabbed our books from our lockers. We had separate classes this morning, so they gave me a quick kiss before they rushed off, their class being on the other side of the school. I lingered at my locker for a minute, admiring the braid they'd put in my hair and double checking to make sure I had all the right classwork.

As I shut my locker and turned to leave, I was met with the nervous face of a girl much shorter than myself, possibly even shorter than Theo. She glanced around quickly, her deep brown eyes darting back and forth. She didn't say a word to me but took my hand and placed a note in it before hurrying off. I glanced down at the note, and by the time I looked back up the girl was completely gone. The bell rang, stopping me from looking at the contents of the paper. Instead, I shoved it in my pocket and ran to my class, just a couple doors down the hallway.

Managing to sit down before the teacher even turned his attention to the class, my curiosity got the better of me. I pulled the note out of my pocket and unfolded it, pressing it flat against my desk.

You don't know me, but you and Theo are pretty well known around the school. I was too nervous to approach them, I figured you'd be safer or more willing to hear me out. I know you guys have had a lot of trouble with bullies because of Theo's gender and both of your sexualities. Our school doesn't have a GSA or anything like that, but a group of us usually meet up after school on Tuesdays. By a group of us I mean 5-6 other queer kids. There's a lot more in the school than you think, we're all just underground. It's easier that way. If you two want, you can meet up with us this afternoon at Best Boba on South Street. You'll both be welcome there, and I feel like you might want the support, since clearly the school isn't giving it to you. You're the only out couple in the school and I see Theo fighting for you both almost every day. So please come if you want.

All the best,

Harriet

I folded the note quickly and shoved it back in my pocket, wondering if this was a trick. I knew there had to be other queer kids in the school, but I'd never met them, excluding Seth. At least, I didn't know if I had. Part of me wanted to go and see. While I'd never really mentally struggled with my sexuality like some people did, it would be nice to have a support system. My mom had ground it into me that it was wrong, but I knew in my heart that it wasn't, and never for a second did I think otherwise. Having some friends that believed the same would feel so good, I'd lost most of my friends when Theo and I became a couple publicly in school. They hadn't been the kind of friends I'd tell all my secrets, so I wasn't shocked when they wanted nothing to do with me after finding out that I was pansexual.

"Alexandra?"

My attention snapped to the front of the room. The teacher was staring in my direction. *Shit, he'd asked me a question.*

The teacher rolled his eyes as I looked at him nervously, giving away that I hadn't heard whatever he'd asked of me. He moved on to the next kid in the class and repeated the question. I tried hard to pay attention through the rest of the class, not wanting to get called out again.

———

At lunch, Theo, Jeremy and I were seated around our table. I glanced at Theo briefly before pulling out the note and sliding it over to them.

"This girl came up to me at my locker and handed me this. Do you think it's legit?"

They inspected the note, reading it over for what felt like an eternity. They glanced up at me quickly and then back down at the note.

"You want to go?"

"Yeah, I mean, if you think it's not a trap."

"Well, she actually used my pronouns, so it's at least a well thought-out trap."

I rolled my eyes, "Seriously, Theo, wouldn't it be nice to have other queer friends? Sam helped you so much, it would be nice to have other people like us around."

Theo bit their lip, mulling it over. It was Jeremy who spoke first, catching me off guard.

"I'm a queer friend, can I come?"

I looked over at him, dumbfounded. "What?"

Theo snorted. "Jeremy likes dudes. Or at least, not-girls."

The two of them exchanged a knowing glance that meant there was more of a story behind what they'd said. I looked between them and leaned in.

"What aren't you telling me?"

Jeremy's face flushed red, and Theo snickered a little, but waved it off. "Nothing. If you want to go, we can go. I'm feeling some bubble tea anyway."

I knew there was something they weren't telling me, but decided to let it go. I'd expected it to be harder to rope Theo into going to the meet-up anyway. At that moment, I felt like I'd won. Satisfied, I picked at the limp salad on my tray. A far cry from anything Seth would've made, but this just had to hold me over until the end of school. Theo bit into the softest sounding apple I'd ever heard, I could almost sympathetically feel the disgusting texture in my mouth. Jeremy had brought a peanut butter and jelly from home. He was eating like a king compared to us.

Speaking of Jeremy, he was pointedly trying not to look at Theo now, and his posture had closed in on itself.

I kicked him lightly under the table. "Okay, seriously, *what?*"

"What do you mean, what?" He wouldn't look at me either.

"Jer, don't try and bullshit her, she knows when shit's up. You're gonna have to let it out of the bag."

He looked up at Theo helplessly and then glanced at me quickly before looking down at his lap. "I kinda… sorta…" and then he mumbled something so low that I couldn't understand him.

"Jeremy, its ridiculously loud in here, you know I didn't hear that." The general buzz of the cafeteria practically drowned out my own thoughts.

"Why do you think we didn't get along at first? Theo really liked you, and I…"

I squinted, the cogs in my brain slowly turning before it hit me.

"Oh my god. Oh my god! You were jealous! You like them!" I exclaimed a little too loud, even for the room.

Jeremy waved his hands in front of me, "Shh, shut up! I get beat on enough here, I don't need people knowing that." His face was now such a deep red it was practically purple.

I put my hand on his shoulder, "Hey, sorry. I just… didn't see that coming. How did I not see that? I always catch things like that."

Jeremy side-eyed me, "Really? *Always?* Theo was literally in love with you for *years.*"

"All right, you've got a point." I looked down and picked at my salad again. "We're cool, right?"

He leaned back a little, seemingly relieved. "Yeah, we're cool. I don't plan on getting between anything. Theo doesn't feel the same way, I'm happy to just be friends."

"How very civil of you two." Theo quipped.

I slapped the back of their hand playfully, "How long did you know? You didn't tell me?"

They shook their head, "It wasn't my place to tell. How would you feel if I went around telling people you're pan?"

"I wouldn't care, but I know that's just me, I get it. You didn't want to out him."

The bell rang and I stood up from the table, nudging Jeremy

with my elbow. "Come with us after school, I'm sure they won't mind a plus one."

He smiled at me, "Okay, but if it is a trap I'm just booking it, no fucks given."

CHAPTER SIX

The three of us approached Best Boba after skipping the bus. It was only about six blocks from the school, not far. It was a pleasant walk, the spring breeze keeping us cool as we went. We paused in front of the window – the shop had a glass front – and I could see the girl from earlier, presumably Harriet, sitting at a table with four other kids. A bell above the door jingled as I took a step inside, and heads turned to see who was walking in. Theo was right behind me, while Jeremy hung back a little, always wary of new situations.

Harriet jumped up from the table. "You came!" She grabbed my hand and led me over to the table, grabbing extra chairs along the way.

"I hope it's okay, we brought a friend. He's cool, he won't tell anyone."

"Yeah!" Her tone was so much more chipper than I'd imagined it would be, voice squeaking a little on the high notes. "The more the better."

Theo approached a chair as Harriet pulled it over, and they brushed hands briefly, causing Harriet's cheeks to flush red in an instant. So that's why she hadn't wanted to give the note to them. Damn, did everyone have a crush on Theo? It's a good thing I didn't get jealous easily.

Theo didn't seem to notice or, if they did, they didn't make a big deal of it. Instead, they briefly placed a hand on my arm. "I'm gonna get a tea, do you want anything?"

I nodded, "Just get me a brown sugar."

They smiled and looked back at Jeremy. "Jer, you want anything?"

He'd barely made his way to the table, looking about as skittish as a feral cat. I'd laugh if I didn't feel bad for the levels of anxiety that were probably coursing through him right then.

"Uh, strawberry." He muttered, so low he could barely be heard.

Theo nodded and left the group to go up to the counter. I plopped down in the seat next to Harriet, and Jeremy timidly took the seat one over, leaving a space for Theo in the middle.

Looking around the group, I was put at ease. While there isn't any one presentation that queer people share, these clearly were not the popular kids or the bullies that would prey on a couple of queer kids. There was Harriet, a very small, non-imposing girl with dark skin and beautiful curls. Next to her was a kid I thought I recognized, but couldn't recall their name. They looked different from what I'd remembered at school, more feminine. Painted nails, brown hair swept forward in a beanie to look like bangs. At the head of the table was a guy I actually recognized from the football team and was slightly shocked to see. He wasn't in the core group of jocks, more on the periphery of the team, usually benched. He was tall, olive skin complementing his hazel eyes. Next was a pale kid with a busted lip, pretty close to matching Jeremy's nervous energy. He wouldn't meet my eyes. Finally, next to Jeremy was a girl with light blond hair and glasses that made her deep blue eyes stand out even more than they normally would.

I made myself at home, taking off my – well, Theo's – hoodie and laying it over the back of the chair, revealing my light green frilly blouse that barely covered my shoulders. Theo returned, three cups of boba in hand, sliding one in front of both me and Jeremy. They took the seat at the end of the table.

That's when Harriet spoke, looking at me. "We know you two from the fights that nearly break out every day, who's this you've brought with you?"

Theo sipped their boba as everyone had their eyes trained on Jeremy. He slouched deeper in the chair. "Uh…"

Theo slapped him lightly with the back of their hand. "You wanted to come! Don't get all shy on us now."

Jeremy took a deep breath and straightened himself in the chair a little, making brief eye contact with Harriet before looking down at the table again.

"We don't bite," Harriet said, a coo in her voice.

"I'm Jeremy." His voice shook.

"Well, Jeremy, I'd kill for your hair," said the person sitting next to Harriet who I still couldn't place.

Jeremy blushed and chuckled, stabbing his straw into the boba and taking a sip. His shoulders relaxed as he leaned into the table.

Harriet smiled, "I'm Harriet, I use she/her pronouns." Then she looked to the person next to her.

"I'm Rachel, I also use she/her pronouns."

It clicked in my head, and before I could stop myself "Rodney!" slipped out of my mouth. Rachel flinched, and I knew I'd fucked up.

"Please don't call me that here," she muttered, looking down at her own tea.

My face started to burn. "I'm so sorry, it's just that I knew I recognized you, I've been trying to figure out how. It won't happen again. Are you not out at school?"

"No, I'm not. No one knows except you all. I still wear guy clothes at school and everything. It kills me, but I'm not a fighter like Theo. I'd never be able to stand up for myself."

"Being a fighter ain't all it's cracked up to be. Sometimes I wish I could just fly under the radar. But I don't envy the dysphoria that comes with trying to pretend." Theo said flatly, swirling their tea around with their straw.

Rachel leaned in. "We all admire you so much, Theo. You and Alex are both so fiercely genuine. We feel like cowards hiding in the background."

"I second that." The guy from the football team said in his rumbling voice. "I'm Brett. He/him. I don't know what I'd do if the team found out about me."

"I got outed this morning," the smaller boy with the busted lip chimed in, "And look where it got me."

Theo and I both squinted at him. "Who did that?"

"The group that's usually after you two, Kyle and his gang."

So *that's* where they'd been this morning. I felt guilty over the relief I'd experienced, knowing now that it came at someone else's expense.

"Anyway, I'm Elliot. I use he/him."

We nodded, and then our eyes turned to the final girl with the glasses. She perked up and bounced in her seat. "Claire, she/her."

"Jeremy, what pronouns do you use?" Harriet asked.

Jeremy paused for a second and squinted, as if the question was difficult. Finally he answered, "He/him?"

The attention turned to Theo just as they were taking a sip of their tea and they almost choked. After an undignified cough they said "They/them."

I smiled as everyone looked at me. Being the center of attention was great when the looks weren't malicious. "She/her."

Harriet smiled, looking around the table. She might've been small, but she was clearly the leader of this little group. She was proud of the community she'd created.

"So…" Theo broke the silence, "What do you all usually do here?"

"We usually just hang out and talk. Before you three got here we were talking about what to do with Elliot's situation." Harriet spoke for the group.

Elliot chimed in. "I'm afraid to go back to school tomorrow. This," he pointed at his lip, "was just a warning shot. it happened right in front of my class and I ran in the room before they could do anything else."

Theo squinted, a flash of anger came behind their eyes. "If you want, you can stick with me and Alex in the mornings. It'll guarantee there will be a hassle if we're all in one place, but you won't get hurt with me there."

Elliot's eyes lit up. "Really? You'd do that?"

Theo nodded, "I've been fighting all my life. It's better to fight for a cause."

I glanced at them and put a hand lightly on their shoulder, "Theo…"

"What? They're gonna come after us anyway, I'll only fight if I have to. I promise I'll keep a handle on it."

I really, really hated them fighting. Hearing them volunteer for it made me nervous. What if they lost control? They'd gotten so much better, I'd hate for them to slip backwards. I studied their face, trying to get a read on how serious they were. They squinted, thinking hard about something.

"Harriet, in your note you said 'there's a lot more of us than you think'. How many more are we talking?" Theo drummed their fingertips on the table, energy ramping up visibly.

Harriet leaned back in her chair, putting her hand up to her chin, "God, I don't know. It's a big school, I don't know *everyone*. But I'd say easily around one hundred."

Theo clapped as they leaned in, causing everyone at the table to lean in as well, "We could… we could do something about this shit."

Harriet backed out of the circle a little. "Theo, that's noble and all, but I don't know. Almost everyone's closeted. You and Alex are the only ones really well known in the school, and everyone sees the shit that you two go through every day. Not many people would sign up for that, and not everyone can fight like you."

"But they wouldn't have to. If there's that many of us, we could shut Kyle and that group down. They're a bunch of pussies anyway, all it takes is a couple punches to send them running – if they knew how many of us there were they'd stop coming back for more. Hell, Brett alone would send them running, they just underestimate me because I'm small."

Brett's face flushed a little before he spoke. "It's not just them, though. Yeah, they're the most aggressive and openly homophobic and transphobic, but I hear off-handed microaggressions constantly every day. It goes a lot deeper than Kyle. If the team found out I'm gay, I'd probably get kicked off."

Now my mind was churning, and I jumped in where Theo had left off. "Then we take it to the school itself. Get them to implement policies to protect us. They can't ignore ten percent of the student population."

"I've tried that," Harriet's voice was resigned, "they said they couldn't do anything without running it by the school board and parent's association, and that killed the number of signatures I could gather on a petition. Half the kids aren't out to their parents either."

"Shit," Theo muttered.

"So we make it anonymous." I didn't skip a beat. "We take a ballot. These policies should be in place anyway, half the schools around here have them."

"And the other half won't let trans kids use the right bathroom," Rachel said defeatedly.

"Look," Harriet leaned back into the huddle we'd created, "If you two can come up with a plan, a real, fully fleshed out plan of action, I'm down to help any way I can. I just want you to know we've tried, and it hasn't gone well. Hatred runs deep in the school, all the way through to the higher ups who hold all the power. We'd have to do something to really tie their hands."

My mind started racing with the possibilities. All the tactics activists had used in the past – rallies, protests, petitions, walk outs. Surely *something* would be viable. The failing in all these options was that the population in the school was so afraid of being outed. There had to be another way, or a way to make people feel safe enough to stand up for themselves. We'd come up with something. We were going to start a *revolution*.

———

After our little meet-up, Jeremy had gone home, unusually silent. We'd all exchanged numbers and agreed to meet up again the following Tuesday. By the time we got back to Theo's house, I was *starving*, having not eaten much at school and barely downing a small bowl of cereal in time for the bus that morning. When we opened the door, I was smacked in the face with the scent of baked macaroni and cheese, barely putting down my backpack before making a break for the kitchen. Theo snickered at me, and Seth looked up as he pulled the pan from the oven.

"Just in time." He placed the pan on the potholders he'd set on the counter.

I raced to grab plates and cutlery, putting them down haphazardly on the counter before taking my fork and sticking it right into the pan.

Seth slapped my hand away. "Damn, let me serve it first." He pulled a large spoon from a drawer and started dishing out food.

Theo appeared next to me a second later, placing a hand on my lower back briefly before pulling some cups from the cupboard. They filled them with filtered water and set them on the counter to go with the food, downing half a cup before even sitting down.

"Tea always makes me so damn thirsty," they muttered before picking up their fork.

I'd already shoved a mouthful of the hot macaroni into my mouth, which had been a mistake. I chewed with my mouth open to try and cool it down as it burned the taste buds on my tongue. Eating Seth's cooking without being able to taste it felt like a crime, so I quickly took a sip of water to try and stop the burning.

What I could taste was *delicious*. I hadn't noticed when he'd been dishing it out, but there was actually lobster in the mac and cheese. It was buttery and had a hint of old bay seasoning on the end. There was just the right balance of cheese to the delicate taste of the lobster. I was a little smarter the second time around and blew on my forkful of food before putting it in my mouth.

I looked next to me and there was Theo, I kid you not, eating *one noodle at a time*. I had to stop myself from laughing for the fear of choking on my mouthful of food. As usual, I finished my plate before anyone else. After downing my glass of water, I took a second helping of the macaroni and dug in. A minute later, Seth finished his food and made a plate for Monica before pointing at the remainder of the food in the pan.

"Either of you going to want more?"

Theo shook their head, and I reluctantly did the same. It was so hard not to overeat when the food was this damn good. Finishing off my second plate, I waited as Theo slowly consumed the last three noodles on their plate. Then I took both of our dishes and set to washing them in the kitchen sink. I slipped into a meditative state, focusing on the warmth of the water and the smell of the dish soap. It was easy to get lost in, enamored by the beautiful colors of the iridescent bubbles that foamed out of the sponge, the soft, almost sizzling sound they made as they popped. I barely noticed when Theo appeared next to me, my body automatically handing dishes over to them to dry before putting them away.

After the last dish was done and I'd come out of my trance, I threw my still damp arms over the back of Theo's neck and kissed them.

"Ew." Their tone was playful, "you've still got dish water all over you!"

I laughed and took the towel they'd been drying the dishes with and rubbed it over my forearms before laying it down on the counter. Seth was already in the living room playing video games, so Theo grabbed me by the hand and pulled me up the stairs. They closed the door behind us and we leaned against it, me kissing Theo up against the hard surface.

After a second, they pulled away. "Fuck."

"What's wrong?" I squinted a little in the darkness of the room.

"I forgot, I have my fucking period. Alex I, I can't. Not now."
Their face fell, there were tears brimming in the corners of their eyes.

"Hey, it's okay. We don't have to do anything. We can just kiss.
Is that all right?"

They walked over to their desk, turning the lamp on before
sitting down in the chair and leaning their elbows on the surface,
their face in their hands.

"I feel so gross. So fucking *wrong*." Their words were muffled,
but I still understood.

I walked over to them, kneeling down on the floor next to the
desk, putting my hands on Theo's knees. "Is this the dysphoria
talking?"

They dropped one of their hands from supporting their face
and placed it on top of one of mine. There was a tear rolling down
their cheek, and I wanted nothing more than to kiss it away.

They sniffled a little before doubling over and quickly moving
their arm against their stomach and muttering, "Fuck."

"Cramps?"

They nodded, their lip quivering as they spoke. "They always
get so much worse when I'm thinking about it."

"Why don't we lie down. I'll go get you a heating pad and some
ibuprofen—wait, fuck, Monica's not home."

"Seth has a key."

"Okay, I'll go bug him for it then, you just lie down."

They got up from the desk slowly, then flopped down on the bed
face first, groaning as they went. I hid the smile that tried to take over
my face – I didn't enjoy their pain, but I always thought it was a little
funny when they resorted to acting like a tired little kid. Pulling their
shoes off, I threw a blanket over them and then went downstairs to
find Seth still on the couch with a controller in his hands.

"Seth?"

He hit pause, "Yeah?"

"Theo said you had a key to the medicine cabinet, can I get some ibuprofen?"

"Yeah, sure." He set down the controller and ran up the stairs before returning a minute later and unlocking the cabinet. "How many?"

"Three. And where do you keep the heating pad?"

"Linen closet in the guest bedroom." He handed me the pills before locking the cabinet back up and returning the key to wherever he'd gotten it from.

I retrieved the heating pad and picked up my backpack along the way before going back upstairs to Theo's room.

"Here, T." I held out the pills.

They sat up gradually, taking the pills and putting them in their mouth before grabbing the water bottle on their shelf and taking a sip. I plugged in the heating pad and handed it to them as well and they put it on their stomach as they lay down again, expelling a puff of air. I pulled my homework from my backpack and climbed over Theo to the other side of the bed with my homework in hand. I was behind. I'd barely done any since what happened with my mom. Every time I sat down to do it, I couldn't focus, and never made any progress towards finishing.

Theo closed their eyes, and I went to pull my phone out of my pocket, then remembered I still didn't have it.

"T, can I use your phone for music? My mom took mine."

Without opening their eyes, they felt around on the shelf above them and then handed me their phone. I pulled up a playlist and connected my headphones, then set to work. I *needed* to get this done.

It was around eleven at night when my focus was broken by Theo groaning loudly enough that I heard it through the headphones. I pulled them off and looked to see Theo, legs over the side of the bed with their head in their hands. They were shaking and rocking back and forth. Reaching out, I placed a hand in the middle of their back and they jumped, turning to look at me.

"What's wrong, T? Do you need anything?"

They wiped their face quickly, trying to hide the tears. "I'm… I'm craving really bad."

"What do you want? I can make you something."

They let out a hollow laugh, "Not that kind of craving, Al."

I squinted, confused. "What do you mean, then?"

An exasperated sigh came out as they turned to me, "Drugs, Alex. I want to use. It hasn't ever been this bad since I was detoxing." They looked away quickly, as if they didn't want to see my reaction.

"*Oh*." I felt naive for not realizing it sooner. "What can I do?"

"Nothing, really. It'll pass. I hope." They flopped back down on the bed, staring at the ceiling, then put their hands over their face.

I lay down next to them, running my hands through their hair. "What's making you want them right now?"

"Everything." They were muffled through their hands, "The dysphoria, everything at school, and I absolutely hate to make it about me but the shit with your mom triggered a lot of stuff for me."

"You're not making it about you, you were there for me when I needed you. Of course it's gonna bring stuff up for you. What happened?"

"I don't know if I ever told you, but one of my homes beat me and sent me away when I said something about liking girls. That's part of why it took me so long to tell you. I was afraid. I knew your mom was like that."

I pulled one of their hands away to get a look at their face, then stroked their hairline, planting a kiss on their forehead. "Do you feel bad about being queer? Because I don't."

They turned to look at me, "Really? I'm not saying you should, but with everything your mom's drilled into you, you don't feel bad at all?"

"Not one bit. You're my world, T, and nothing is wrong with that. Nothing's wrong with you."

"I feel bad all the time. I don't know how you do it, with so many people telling you you're just *wrong*. And then how my body feels right now, it's hard not to feel like there's something wrong with me. I get so much dysphoria from so many things, then my period comes along and makes it worse. I hate my body. I hate almost everything about myself."

Tears brimmed in my eyes, it broke my heart to hear them talk like this. "Hey, don't talk about my partner like that. They're too good to be hated."

They let out a sigh, and then placed a hand on the back of my head, pulling me in for a kiss. "You're too good for me, you know that?"

"I'm not," I smiled into them. "But I appreciate the sentiment."

I pulled away after the kiss, and Theo tucked a stray piece of hair behind my ear, their hand lingering on my jawline. Their touch was so warm, and I wanted more, but knowing how they felt then I didn't want to make any advances. Instead, I mirrored their touch, running a hand through their hair and around their jawline.

Theo sat up, groaning as they went, then looked over at the pile of papers next to us. "Shit, you're still doing homework? I'm sorry

I interrupted you."

"You're not an interruption." I lightly tapped their arm. "I'm almost done, anyway. Just a little bit of math left."

"Okay, you finish. I'm gonna get in the shower, maybe I'll feel less gross afterwards."

"Yeah, after we can cuddle and watch cartoons or something until we fall asleep."

They gave me a faint smirk, then got up to get clothes out of their dresser. Then they left me in the dimly lit room to finish my work alone.

CHAPTER SEVEN

In the morning, Theo wasn't much better. They were pretty much silent, a sullen look on their face. I tried my best to cheer them up, making jokes with Seth and helping them get ready, but nothing seemed to help. I saw them take an extra dose of their as-needed medication before we even left for school.

Elliot met us as soon as we walked into the school. He'd been pacing at the entrance before we walked up. I'd forgotten about the plan for him to stick with us, and my stomach began to twist into knots at the thought of a confrontation right now. Theo wasn't in the best state of mind, and I had no idea how they would handle Kyle and his friends today. When they were this withdrawn, they could snap quickly and things could get out of hand.

Elliot smiled at us. I smiled back, and Theo gave an understanding nod of their head. We walked into the school and were immediately encroached upon by Kyle and his group. They'd been waiting.

"Hey, the pussy finally decided to come inside!" Kyle jeered.

Elliot visibly shrunk a little, taking a step closer to me and Theo.

"Oh, we needed a bodyguard, did we? Pathetic." Kyle reached for Elliot. He was an easier target than Theo. He knew Elliot wouldn't fight back.

Kyle's hand that was trained for Elliot's arm was stopped short by Theo's grasp.

"Fuck off Kyle, not today." Their voice was a low growl, I could already hear the tension in their tone, threatening to snap.

"Let go of me, you freak!" Kyle jerked his hand away.

Elliot took a step behind Theo, and I instead stepped in front of them.

"Kyle, seriously, not today."

With me in front of Theo, Kyle took the opportunity he rarely got to harass me directly. He grabbed me by the wrist and reached around to put a hand on my butt. I twisted to avoid him, and there was Theo, temper out the window. They grabbed him by the shoulders and shoved him down to the ground roughly. They lifted up a leg to give him a swift kick in the stomach, but stopped when I put my hands around their waist.

"T, don't."

They looked at me, eyes wide in anger and tears brimming around the edges. They weren't okay. I knew they didn't want to break in front of this guy, but they were so close to it that their options were white hot anger or a breakdown. I had to get them away.

I leaned in, whispering into their ear, "We're going to the nurse."

They nodded, and I tapped Elliot on the shoulder to follow us.

Kyle slowly lifted himself from the ground, shouting obscenities behind us as we turned away. Every fiber of my being was terrified that they'd come after us. If Theo got pushed again I could only see a disaster. Theo was shaking violently, and I knew they wouldn't be able to stop the next impulse. Elliot looked worried, glancing between us and the group of bullies, and he didn't even know how dire the situation could become if it got any further.

I kept my arm around Theo's shoulders, trying to ground them. Thankfully, Kyle didn't seem keen on pursuing us. He had turned his back on us, holding the shoulder he'd landed on like it hurt. Theo had shoved him pretty hard. Looking back at Theo, I could see the tears trying to force their way out and how hard Theo was trying to hold them back.

We got to the nurse just as Theo completely lost their composure and a sob escaped their body. The nurse rushed over to us and helped me guide Theo to the couch. They sat down, hands shaking and breath ragged. I sat next to them and they collapsed into me.

"Do you need your medication, hun?" the nurse asked, kneeling in front of us.

"They just took one this morning before we got here. They can't have another yet, can they?" I rubbed Theo's back as they shook, unable to answer.

"Oh, no, I'm afraid not." She turned back to Theo, "Hun, what do you need from us? Do you need to go for a run on the track? I can give you a pass."

Theo clung to me with all their strength, squeezing my waist tight. Eventually, they managed, "I… I… need to leave."

"Do you want me to call your mom?"

Theo nodded, and the nurse went behind her desk to make the phone call. I held them, stroked their hair and kissed their forehead. Elliot was still standing in the doorway of the nurse's station, unsure of what to do with himself. He glanced between us and the nurse, trying to understand what was happening.

The nurse returned and knelt in front of us again. "She's on her way, it'll only be a few minutes."

The bell rang loudly, causing Theo to nearly jump off the couch. I squeezed them tighter, "Shh, it's okay. You're safe."

Putting a hand on my shoulder, the nurse turned to me. "Alex, you should get to class. I'll take care of them from here."

Reluctantly, I moved my hands from Theo's back to their arms, slowly prying them off of me. They were shaking so hard, I felt so bad for leaving them, even though I had no choice. They let go and looked up at me, their face flushed and wet with tears. I took their face in my hands and kissed them one last time. "I'll see you when I get home, okay? Go get some rest."

They nodded, curling in on themself, their whole body shaking so violently I swear the couch moved a little. I got up, looking back at Theo warily the whole time. I met Elliot at the door before turning back and telling Theo "I love you."

Elliot struggled to keep up with my brisk pace as we walked down the hallway, "Are they gonna be okay?" He kept stealing glances back towards the nurse's office.

"Yeah," a sigh in my tone, "they just need to rest. They haven't been doing very well the past couple days."

"What's wrong?" Concern laced his voice.

A pang of guilt hit me, they wouldn't want all this out in the open. I shook my head, "It's not my place to say. When you get to know them better, you'll know."

"Oh, okay." Thankfully, Elliot accepted the answer. He glanced around the hallway, as if waiting for people to jump out at him. "How are we gonna get to class now? Kyle's probably still in the hallway."

"Where's yours? There's a shortcut to mine through the teacher's lounge, they let me go through sometimes."

"Mine's up the stairs just past where they were hanging out."

"Shit," I muttered.

We slowed as we came up on the hallway where the group had

been, and one of them spotted us before we could sneak by. They descended upon us so quickly we didn't have time to race up the stairs away from them, or to split up for our classes. We were surrounded.

Kyle came forward, hand still on his injured shoulder as he rolled it. "What are you little bitches gonna do now that Liz's not here?" His smirk was every bit as menacing as his tone. It wasn't even my deadname, but it hit me like a ton of bricks.

I stood in front of Elliot, trying to protect him, but I heard him yelp as someone behind us grabbed him. I turned around to try and help, but someone grabbed me by the shoulders and pulled me back as well. They held us there as Kyle took another step forward, just inches from me.

"It would be a shame to mess up that pretty face of yours, so I guess," he punched me hard in the stomach, knocking the breath from me. I gasped as he held my chin up with his free hand, "I'll have to hit you somewhere else, slut." Coughs came out of me as I tried to reclaim the air in my lungs and Kyle turned to Elliot. "You, on the other hand, you already look like shit." He punched Elliot in the nose, and I heard a crack when his fist collided with Elliot's face. I struggled against whoever was holding me to try and help him, but I couldn't get away, I was helpless, hopeless. There was nothing I could do. We were fucked.

Unless…

I glanced at the door to the classroom closest to us, the bell had rung already for classes to begin, so the teacher was sure to be inside. It was Theo's English class, the only teacher in the school that I absolutely knew would do something.

I screamed. Loud.

Kyle put his hand over my mouth as quickly as he could, "Shh, shut up, bitch!"

The door opened a second later, and Kyle and his group made a run for it. Elliot dropped to the ground, coughing as blood ran down from his nose. I knelt down, putting a hand on his back and tried to get a look at his face to assess the damage.

Theo's English teacher rushed over to us. "Alex, what's going on?"

I sucked in air, breath still ragged from the punch. Then, I looked up at the teacher, "They were holding us so they could beat on us. I think they broke Elliot's nose."

The teacher knelt down next to us, lifting Elliot's chin gently with her hand. Elliot winced, unable to look the teacher in the eyes.

"Damn," she muttered, "Who did this?"

"Kyle and his group. They're always after us, Theo usually runs them off, but Theo needed to go home today."

"I see." She helped Elliot to his feet, "Elliot, you go see the nurse. Alex, you should get to class. Are you all right?"

"Yeah, just got the wind knocked out of me."

"Okay. I'll see what I can do about this. It's absolutely unacceptable."

The anger in her eyes reminded me of Theo. Justified rage at everything wrong in the world. It wasn't for us, it was for everyone trying to keep us down. She watched Elliot and I go in our separate directions, then turned to return to her class.

As I walked into my math class, the teacher tapped an impatient foot and stared daggers in my direction while I walked to my desk. "Any particular reason you're just now joining us, Alexandra?"

Damn, I was only five minutes late.

I just stared at him. I knew a truthful explanation wouldn't get me anywhere, this guy was historically an ass. Ignoring him, I pulled my math book from my backpack and plopped it on my desk, making a thudding noise that could be heard from the next room. I didn't care. I was so done with today already. The teacher rolled his eyes at me, then turned back to the board and began the lesson. He was reviewing the homework, so I dug through my bag to pull it out before realizing I'd never finished the night before. There were only two problems left, so I quickly scrawled my way through them while the teacher droned on. I'd been falling behind in math recently. It was the subject I struggled most with. These damn problems took me *so long*.

"Alexandra?"

My head snapped up to look at the teacher, who had undoubtedly asked me something.

"Care to come do this one on the board?"

He was calling me out, trying to embarrass me for being late. Slowly, I stood up from my desk and grabbed a piece of chalk and started to write the problem out. There were a few snickers behind me, and I knew I'd gone wrong somewhere.

"No, no, no. Let me show you." He took the chalk from my hand and erased my work, quickly making his way through the problem. With a final tap of the chalk on the board, he put it down and then looked at me, smug as ever. "See? Simple."

I sat back down at my desk, defeated. This day wasn't going to get any better.

––––––––––

At lunch, I looked around, trying to find Elliot and check up on him. I didn't see him anywhere, so I sat at our usual table, across from Jeremy. He looked around quizzically while I pulled out Theo's phone that they'd handed me before I left the nurse's office and sent Elliot a text to check in.

You okay? I can't find you here at lunch. (It's Alex)

They sent me out to the hospital for x-rays. Pretty sure it's broken.

Shit, I'm sorry. Let me know if there's anything I can do.

It's not on you, you at least got them off me. See you tomorrow?

Of course.

I looked up from the phone to see Jeremy staring at me. "Where's Theo?" he asked, playing with the cold French fries on his tray.

"They had to go home. They're not doing great. I'm worried." I stared down at my overcooked burger, not even wanting to touch it.

"How worried are we?" He leaned in, almost whispering.

"Like a six. Jer, they told me they wanted to use last night. I know they're doing everything they can, but with them home I'm afraid they'll slip."

"I think you gotta give them a little more credit than that. Saying they want to is a lot different from them actually doing it."

"Yeah, I just… worry. They've been struggling a lot lately. Not as bad as when they… you know. But it's the worst it's been in a while. They almost lost it this morning."

"We just gotta support them together. I know you do everything you can, but it's not all on you, you know?"

I nodded, acknowledging Jeremy's support, but still feeling just as much pressure on myself. Looking down at my phone, I noticed a text from Monica.

Elliot came to the office with a bloody nose before Mom picked me up, are you okay?

It must've been Theo on Monica's phone since they lent me theirs. I didn't tell them I'd gotten hit. They'd only feel guilty that they hadn't been there to help.

I'm fine, how are you doing?

I'm okay, I took a nap and a hot shower and I feel a little bit better. Miss you.

I miss you too, I'll see you at home. Love you.

Love you too.

I was glad to know that they were doing a little bit better, but the nagging feeling of worry still clouded my mind. I wanted nothing more than to go home and be with them, to take care of them.

My attention snapped up as I felt Jeremy's hand on my shoulder, a light touch.

"Alex, seriously. You put too much pressure on yourself. You're not responsible for everything they do."

I sighed, putting the phone down on the table and dropping my head into my hands. Normally, I handled stress well, easily hiding it from everyone. Apparently, I'd met my limit in the past week. Focusing on my breathing, I took in air and held it for a few seconds before releasing it. I looked down at the tray, the sight of food making me nauseous. This had never happened before, and I was starting to get afraid that I was sick or something. I pushed the tray away from me and Jeremy offered me a sympathetic look.

Suddenly, all the scents in the cafeteria were too much. I got up from the table, making a run for the nearest bathroom. I barely made it to an open stall before throwing up everything I'd eaten that day. The only other time I'd felt like this was the night that Theo had attempted suicide. I didn't know what to do with myself. I was shaking as I sat back against the stall wall and tried desperately to take some deep breaths.

Someone came out of the stall next to me, and I realized I'd left the door open. I scrambled to shut it, but before I could I was met by the face of Harriet. She turned and washed her hands without a word, but then came back and knelt next to me.

"Hey, are you okay? You don't look good."

My hands shook uncontrollably, and I placed them on top of my knees to try and stop it. "I… I don't think so." Tears forced their way into my eyes and I couldn't stop them from spilling out and running down my face.

"Okay, hey, where's Theo? Can I get them for you?"

"They had to go home. We had a run-in with Kyle this morning. Elliot's got a broken nose."

"Shit. That's… shit." She sat back against the stall wall with me.

My ribs hurt. I didn't know why. All the sensations in my body felt like they were dialed up to ten. It was as if I could feel my blood pumping through my veins, too fast. My lungs unable to expand all the way, my heart thumping against my chest, trying to escape.

I couldn't stop it as bile rose up in my throat, and I rushed to the toilet to throw up again, nothing but acid and spit. Harriet pulled my hair out of the way just in time, then placed a hand gently on my back.

"Maybe you should go to the nurse."

"No, I can't, they'll call my mom."

"Is that bad?"

"Yes. I'm…" I wasn't sure if we were close enough yet for me to tell her everything, but it was coming out of my mouth now and there was no stopping it. "I'm staying at Theo's. My mom hurt me when she found out we were dating. She said she wants to send me to a conversion camp. They can't call her, she'll send me away. I don't think I'd survive it."

"Shit, a fucking conversion camp? She's serious?"

I nodded, then buried my face in my knees, taking in ragged breaths. Now she was the only one that knew other than Theo and Monica.

She put an arm around my shoulders. Then the bell rang, making me jump and upsetting my stomach all over again. I had nothing left to throw up, and I dry heaved over the toilet as Harriet pulled my hair back one last time.

"Can't you tell them? I know this school sucks about this stuff, but if your mom hurt you I'm sure they have to do something, by law."

"No!" I said, louder than I'd meant to, "No, I can't. They'll call child protective services or something like that. I can't risk them taking my little sister away from her. I'd be putting her through hell over something she has nothing to do with."

"If your mom hurt you, how do you know she wouldn't hurt your little sister? Maybe it's best if people get involved."

"Harriet, do you know anything about the foster system?" My tone sounded angrier than I'd intended, but all that was flashing through my head was the horror stories I'd heard from Theo, and I was sure there was more they hadn't told me.

She shook her head solemnly, biting her lip.

"It's not a good place, Harriet. Only lucky kids get the good homes, and my sister's deaf. She wouldn't be the first kid that people would pick. More fucked up shit happens in the system than my mom could ever do. My mom would never hurt Leah, ever. She's the perfect child to her. I'm not going to risk her getting put somewhere where she might actually get hurt for my own sake."

Harriet nodded, accepting my rant as the end of the discussion. But then she added, "You deserve to be safe too."

"I'm safe at Theo's. No one will hurt me there." I ran my hands along my arms, goosebumps dotting my skin. I had to get this panic under control, compose myself and go to class. I couldn't risk anything the school would call my mom over.

Taking a deep breath, I stood up, wobbly at first. Steadying myself against the wall of the stall, I took the few steps forward to the sink and hunched over it, turning it on. I washed my mouth out to get rid of the taste of acid, then splashed cold water on my face. The coldness of the water slowed the bile rising in my throat again. Harriet got up and met me at the sink with a couple paper towels in hand. I took them from her and patted my face dry. Looking in the mirror was a mistake, I looked like shit. My makeup was smudged, mascara and eyeliner creating a raccoon-like look. I didn't have time to fix it, so I tried to scrub it off with the paper towels, rubbing my eyes raw. I managed to get most of it off, then turned as Harriet put a hand on my shoulder.

"I'll walk you to your class."

"You'll be late for yours, you don't have to."

"It's fine, I have homeroom next, they don't care if you're a little late. I want to make sure you actually get there and don't collapse in the middle of a hallway somewhere."

"Okay." I relented. It didn't seem like she was going to take no for an answer.

———

When the bus dropped Seth and I off at home, I made a beeline for Theo's room. Once I was inside, I shut the door behind me and fell to the ground as sobs overtook my body. I lost the barely put-together composure I'd feigned throughout the rest of the school day. It had been cracking little by little, more each class. I was almost impressed I'd managed to hold it together until I got home.

It was dark in the room, but I heard soft talking coming from the only light source – Theo's laptop. They were watching some silly sitcom. Or rather, had fallen asleep watching it. They stirred in bed as my sobs grew louder, then shot upwards when they woke up. Immediately, they were out of the bed and kneeling down in front of me, hands on my shoulders. I fell into them, burying my face in their chest.

"Jesus, Al, what's wrong?" They started easing the backpack I'd forgotten to put down off my shoulders and then wrapped their arms around my back, pulling me in closer.

I couldn't speak, the sobs were coming too hard. I just clung to Theo and cried, unable to do anything else. They rubbed my back, and when I didn't stop after ten minutes they pulled away slightly.

"C'mon, come get in bed." They eased my shoes off, then helped me to my feet.

I was breathing erratically through the sobs and leaned on them as they walked me over to the bed where I collapsed, wincing in pain as I hit my side on the mattress. Theo left my side for a minute, and then there was some light in the room as they turned the desk lamp on. They came back and noticed me holding my side with a grimace as the sobs shook my entire body.

"Allie, what happened?"

I still couldn't answer. It was hard enough to breathe.

They lifted my shirt, revealing a dark bruise on my ribs I hadn't realized was there. Dropping my blouse back down, they got up and started pacing the room.

"Fuck, fuck! I shouldn't have left. I should've been there to protect you. Did Kyle do that? Why didn't you tell me?"

They continued pacing, hands at their temples as stress visibly made its way through their body. They hit their head with the heels of their palms, their breathing starting to race as they walked between the bed and the door.

I needed to say something before they spiraled. *Anything.*

"T," barely came out, overcome by a sob at the same time. It was enough to get their attention, and they stopped and walked over to the bed and knelt down in front of me. Their breath felt warm against my skin, coming in fast, erratic puffs. We were both losing it. This was going to go bad quickly, we were both about to break.

I put a shaky hand on the back of their head, running my fingers through their hair. The softness was soothing. It gave me something to focus on and seemed to be grounding them a bit too.

"Al, please stop crying. I don't know what to do." Their voice was small and broke at the end of the phrase.

It had been about twenty minutes of sobbing at this point, and I was *exhausted*. I tried to take deep breaths that kept getting interrupted by my body heaving with each sob. Theo's hands shook as they touched my face, trying to wipe away the flood of tears. They sat back on their heels, thinking for a minute before looking towards their dresser.

"Okay, Al, don't be mad."

What was I going to be mad about? My mind raced as Theo walked over to their dresser, opening the bottom drawer. Did they actually go out and score drugs today, like I'd feared? I used all my strength to sit up and see what they were doing, still crying. My hands desperately tried to wipe away the tears that blurred my vision. Then it hit me as Theo pulled a small shoebox out of their bottom drawer. *The smell.* It was like they'd just unleashed a herd of skunks into the room. It wasn't heroin. It was *weed*.

They brought the box up to the bed and opened their window before pulling out a bag of bud, a grinder, and some rolling papers. Their hands were quick and practiced, making short work of splitting up and grinding the weed into fine powder. Then they tapped the powder out on the rolling paper, licking an edge as they rolled it up into a neat joint. I watched every move they made, leaning back against the wall as the sobs started to slow down. They pulled a lighter out of the box and raised the joint to their lips, taking in a deep breath as they lit the end of it. They blew the smoke out the window, then reached their arm out, offering me the joint.

"It'll help," they said, searching my face for a reaction.

I'd never smoked before in my life. I wasn't even sure how to. I took the joint in my hand, then looked up at them as my hand shakily raised the joint to my lips. I hesitated.

"It's okay if you don't want to, I'm not gonna force you, that'd be fucked up." They put a hand on my shoulder.

"I just… I don't know how."

They chuckled a little. "You're too innocent for me, you know that?" They took my hand in theirs, steadying it as they helped bridge the gap between the joint and my lips. "Take a deep breath in through it, ou're gonna want to cough—"

I was already coughing, hacking hard as the smoke seared my lungs. How did people *do* this? Theo made it look so smooth, so graceful.

Theo laughed, taking the joint from my hands and another drag off of it. They rubbed my back as I continued coughing, making an absolute fool of myself. At least Theo was the only one around to see it. Once I finally got some air in my lungs, I felt light-headed. I wasn't sure if it was from the weed or all the coughing.

Theo held out the joint again. "Try again, don't take such a big hit this time. Just take a little and then try and hold it for a second before you blow it out."

I took the joint, hands shaking considerably less. Taking the tiniest breath in, I held it for a split second before the coughs started coming hard and fast again. This time, after a few coughs I felt a head rush, my eyes squinting a little as I breathed in and out while Theo took another hit.

I started giggling. "You make it look so easy."

"Al, I've been smoking since I was thirteen."

"What?" I knew they'd started self-medicating young, but not *that* young.

"C'mon, it's no different than you losing your virginity at thirteen. We've both got our shit."

I couldn't argue with them there. Instead, I rolled my eyes and reached out for the joint again.

Theo hesitated, "This should be your last one for now, just until we see how you do with it."

I nodded and took the joint, trying another small inhale. This time, I managed to hold it in longer and only coughed a little, small puffs of smoke coming out of my mouth each time. Handing the joint back to Theo, I leaned into them, resting my head on their shoulder. They put their hand on my temple and kissed my forehead before taking another drag.

Closing my eyes, it felt like the room was moving around me. I gave in to the feeling and let myself float there, tension falling away from my muscles. My body felt completely exhausted, like if I tried to move I wouldn't be able to, I'd just be stuck there. I did feel calmer. I wasn't sure if it was from the weed or crying for half an hour straight. At this point, I didn't really care. I let my body relax into Theo, letting them support my full weight as they stubbed out what little was left of the joint. They closed the window behind us and then leaned back against it, resting their head on mine.

I sighed, letting the calm wash over my body. After this week, I never thought I'd feel this relaxed again. I did feel better, all the things that had been racing through my head during the day fell away. Simply being there with Theo was all I needed in the moment. I was free, I was happy, I was…

So hungry.

My stomach growled loudly and my brain yearned for every junk food that I could think of. "Do we have any snacks?" I asked, not even opening my eyes.

Theo gently pushed me off of them, leaning me against the wall. Then they disappeared, only to return a minute later with a bag of cheese puffs. They handed me the bag that I struggled to open, whining childishly after the third or fourth attempt. I'd lost track. They laughed and opened the bag for me, putting it between us as I leaned back on them. I pulled out a cheese puff and stuffed it into my mouth.

It was *so good.* Like, unreasonably good for a generic snack. I wanted the whole bag in my mouth immediately. I pulled another one out and inspected every inch of the cheesy goodness, turning it around just inches from my face. I'd had these cheese puffs before, how did I never notice how absolutely delicious they were? I stared at it for what felt like an eternity, looking at each crack on its surface and how the cheese dust sat on each part of the crisp.

"What are you doing?" Theo broke my concentration.

"I'm… They're *so good.* Why are they so good?" Tears brimmed in my eyes, threatening to spill out over my face again.

Theo rolled their eyes and shoved the cheese puff in my mouth. "You're high."

I reveled in the buttery, cheesy goodness as I shoved cheese puff after cheese puff into my mouth, and before I knew it, the whole bag was gone. Theo had only taken a few. And I was still hungry.

"Can we get more snacks?"

"So you get the munchies, noted." Theo chuckled as they left the room again and returned with a bag of Doritos and a bag of pretzel chips.

I snatched the already open bag of Doritos from them and shoved a handful into my mouth, leaning back on Theo as they got comfortable in the bed. They pulled their laptop in front of them and hit play on the sitcom they'd been watching.

I swear I fell asleep with my hand in the Doritos bag, cheese powder all over my face.

CHAPTER EIGHT

It was Saturday. The rest of the school week had been lonely, Theo stayed home Thursday and Friday, even though they felt guilty about not being there to protect me. They needed the break, to recoup mentally. I kept telling them *I'm fine, I'll be fine.* Not really believing it myself. Elliot and I had strategically met up in front of school and dodged Kyle's group by sneaking through adjacent classrooms before anyone was in class. Yes, his nose was broken, his face was bruised, deep purple spreading beneath his eyes. He wore it like a champ, but my anger grew as it seemed like Kyle wasn't getting any consequences for what he'd done.

"There weren't any witnesses," the guidance counselor said, as if the word from the two of us wasn't enough to implicate a kid that was known for bullying. Elliot said his mother was furious, threatening to go to the school board with pictures of his face and a call to action. I said she should, maybe light a fire under them to actually do something for us. We shouldn't have to literally fight our way through the hallways just to get to our classes.

Today, though, Theo had me at the gym, standing in front of a punching bag, learning how to pick up that fight for myself.

"I can't always be there. I want you to know how to defend yourself. Show me what you know," they said solemnly.

I nodded, staring at the bag without any clue of what to do. I raised a fist and punched the bag as hard as I could, barely making it wobble.

Theo looked at me blankly. "Really?"

"I've never fought, Theo, I don't know shit. I spend all my time pulling you off of people."

"Okay, well first, you've gotta keep your thumb on the outside. If you punch with it inside your fist, you can break it."

I looked down at my hand and adjusted my fingers so that my thumb was outside of my fist, then held it up to Theo. "Like this?"

"Yes. Now, when you go to punch someone, you've got to lean in a little, throw your weight into it. Where should you punch someone coming at you?"

"I don't know, the face?"

"No. Faces are all bone, unless you've got a lot of power behind your punch it's bound to hurt your hand more than their face. Go for soft spots. If you hit them in the stomach right you'll knock the wind out of them and it'll give you enough time to get away. Like this."

They balled their hand into a fist, dropping it low and then leaning in to punch upward into the bag, causing it to knock back. They caught the bag and then turned to me.

"Now you try."

Taking a deep breath, I stepped up to the bag, made a fist and dropped it low just as they had. Then, with all my strength, I punched upwards, making the bag wobble considerably more than I had the first time.

"Good! Go again."

I laid out a few more punches, feeling more confident with each one. I imagined Kyle's snarky face with each succeeding punch. It actually felt kind of good.

"Okay, what if someone grabs you?"

"Uh…" I stood there with no clue, until Theo came up behind me and locked their arms around my waist and arms.

"What can you do?" They whispered into my ear.

My concentration broke as my spine tingled at their whispers. I loved it when they got this close with me, it was intoxicating. I breathed in their scent, every fiber of my being wanted to turn around and kiss them.

No. I needed to focus. They were on their tiptoes to reach me the way they were, it would be easy to knock them off balance if I just…

I jerked around, trying to turn, and surprisingly, they didn't budge, they held me firmly in place.

"Elbows."

I squinted, looking down at my arms and then bending them, jabbing backwards slightly and colliding with Theo's ribs. They let me go and stepped backwards and doubled over with a slight squeak.

"Shit, did I hurt you?" I turned around, laying a hand on their shoulder and bending down to see their face.

They laughed. "No, I'm good. You've got that one down. Now kicks."

Theo stepped back up to the bag and gave it a swift sideways kick, making it swing wildly on its chain. They stopped it with their hands before turning back to me. I stepped up in a similar fashion, kicking the bag with all my force. It didn't fly as far as Theo had made it go, but it still felt pretty good.

"Don't be afraid to kick them in the balls. If anyone deserves a good kick to the privates it's Kyle, especially in a situation where it's you that has to do it. I know you won't be as quick to action as I am, your brain isn't always in fight mode. It'll take an actually dire situation before you're the one doing it."

I nodded, then kicked the bag straight-on, sending it flying backwards while imagining Kyle's face twist in surprise as I showed him I couldn't be so easily taken down.

"He'll never see it coming." Theo smiled.

We were there for probably an hour, me just beating on this punching bag, making it move a little bit more each time. Theo guided me through everything, gentle and calm at each turn. When we were done, I was ungracefully sweaty and out of breath, but felt empowered. Not that I was going to go around punching everyone I didn't like from now on, but now I had some defense to keep noses from getting broken the next time we were cornered.

We went to the locker room and Theo threw me a towel to dry off with. "What do you want to do for the rest of the day?" they asked.

"Can we get me a new phone? I don't want to have to take yours all the time."

"Yeah, we can get one of those no-contract ones so you don't have to get on a plan."

"Can we go to the mall to get it? What about a spa day at the salon?"

"You're nuts if you think I'm letting anyone paint my nails."

I bumped them with my shoulder. "You don't have to, you can just sit with your legs in the foot bath thing. Tell me you've never done that?"

They shook their head. "Never."

"Ooh, this is gonna be fun!" I squealed after sufficiently wiping the sweat from my face and fixing my hair back into a neat ponytail.

Grabbing their hand, I yanked them out of the locker room and we made our way outside to the fresh spring air. There was a slight breeze, sweet smelling and helping to cool me down after that workout. I laced my fingers between Theo's and they smiled up at me. We bumped shoulders, leaning into each other as we walked. I needed this, something to take my mind off everything.

We approached the mall and went to the department store first, selecting me a cheap new phone with a card plan. It wasn't much, but I didn't have any money and Theo was gracious enough to let me get the phone I'd picked out. I'd been careful about the price. I didn't want to take all their money. After we activated it, I put in Theo's number and then most of Theo's contacts – Jeremy, Seth, Harriet, the whole group. I texted everyone to let them know it was me. It was a hassle, but it felt good to be easily connected with everyone again.

I shoved the phone in my pocket and then dragged Theo to the spa that took up two storefronts in the mall. They were reluctant, but I asked for a manicure for myself and a foot bath for both of us, then Theo asked if they could get their hair touched up. The woman at the desk was pleasant and quickly ushered us into chairs – me at the nail salon section and Theo for their hair. We'd have seats next to each other for the foot baths.

The woman doing my nails was big, loud, and kind in a way I'd never seen. She would've been intimidating were it not for the huge smile on her face as she sat down in front of me at her station.

"What're we lookin' to do today?" She asked loud enough that I was sure the whole mall heard her.

I looked down at my hands. The skin was dry and cracking, my nails raggedy and uneven from me chewing on them. My cuticles were overgrown and torn. I'd been neglecting myself a lot the last few weeks, and it showed when you looked close. I grunted, not having realized how bad of shape my hands were in.

"I dunno, can you fix this?" I held up my hands.

She took my right hand with a firm but gentle grasp and turned my hand over before looking at the left hand in the same fashion. "It looks like we're going to need the full experience. Are you up for that? Your nails will end up kind of short unless we use gel or acrylics, what would you like to do?"

"It's okay if they're short, just, better than this."

The woman nodded and then led me over to a huge wall covered in little shelves of nail polish. "Pick your color, hun."

A shimmery emerald green caught my eye, but it was on the top shelf. I stretched on my tiptoes to try and reach it, but my hand could only make it to the shelf below what I actually wanted.

"Which one are you going for?" The woman came over next to me, easily six inches taller than myself.

"The green one, please." I pointed, still on my tiptoes.

The woman plucked the polish from the shelf with little effort and then led me back to her station. She got to work on my hands quickly, filing down dry skin and nails.

"You seem like a pretty well put together girl, how'd your hands get so bad?"

I wasn't expecting this to get so personal so quickly. "I, uh… It's been a rough couple of weeks."

"How so?" she asked, not looking up from my nails.

I winced a little as she pushed back my cracked and dry cuticles.

"I'm…" I stopped, not wanting to dump all my issues on this poor unsuspecting nail technician.

She paused and looked up at me. "Hun, I like making people feel better outside and inside if I can. Nothing you say here goes anywhere. I'm a safe and willing set of ears."

I released the breath I'd been holding since the last question. She seemed kind enough, and she was right. Even if she told her whole crew what I said, so what? It was a bunch of strangers that might never see me again.

"I'm pansexual, and my mom's a Bible thumper. She found out I was with my partner and kicked me out of the house. Not to mention school." My leg bounced in place, nerves rising up in me at the memory of my mom confronting Theo on that sidewalk.

"What's going on at school?"

"There's this group of bullies, they go after the queer kids mostly. They broke my friend's nose and bruised my ribs pretty badly. The school won't do shit about it." I glanced around when the curse found its way out of my mouth, looking for tiny ears that shouldn't hear it. "...Sorry, I didn't mean to curse."

She waved a hand at me, "No worries, hun, that sounds like exactly the right situation to curse in."

"My partner – Theo – spent the whole morning teaching me how to fight so I can defend myself at school. I wish it wasn't like this. We shouldn't have to fight in order to just live our lives."

"Life *is* fighting, hun. We're fighting every day, even if we don't realize it. But everyone gets tired at some point, and it sounds like things have been piling on for you."

I slouched a little in the chair, careful not to move my hands as she applied the polish to my freshly cut and filed nails. "I'm exhausted."

"Then a little spa day is just what you need." The woman nodded at me, waving her hand above my nails to help them dry quicker.

Theo appeared next to me a few minutes later, sporting a trimmed haircut with a couple fade lines shaved into the sides. They sat down in the vacant chair next to me.

"Ooh, T, you look so good!" I fawned, resisting the urge to run my hand through their hair with my freshly painted nails.

They smiled and peered over the desk at my nails, "I like that color, it's like your eyes." They leaned over and kissed my cheek.

"This must be Theo," the nail technician said, sitting back and waiting for my nails to fully dry before applying a top coat. "Aren't you a cute couple?" Her smile was genuine, not a hint of judgment to be found.

Theo smiled nervously, as if unsure of what to make of this woman. They were usually a pretty good judge of character, but I'd noticed that they were intimidated by people who had them severely outclassed in size. This woman was easily three Theos put together. The woman gave Theo the same warm smile she'd given me at the start, and I saw the tension visibly drop from their shoulders.

The nail technician applied a shimmery top coat to my nails, then leaned back in her chair. "How about we get you two set up at the foot spa?"

She led us over to a row of massage chairs with small pools of water at the feet. I settled into my chair, careful not to touch anything with my still drying nails. Theo plopped in the seat next to me, then jumped forward slightly as the motors in the chair turned on.

"What the fuck?" They squirmed, leaning forward so that their back didn't touch the chair.

I giggled. "They're massage chairs, Theo. You're telling me you've never been in one?"

Theo shook their head, turning around to poke at the contraption.

I leaned over and pushed Theo back in the chair, their back making contact with the seat. They shivered at first, then started to relax. The same woman that had done my nails sat at my feet and started pulling off my shoes and socks and placed my feet into the warm water. Theo took off their own footwear and then put their feet into the bath.

"This is so weird," they muttered.

"C'mon," I prodded them with my elbow, "Let loose a little, relax. Let someone take care of you for once."

They rolled their eyes and leaned back in the chair. I laughed at them.

———

After the spa, Theo had insisted on getting one of those giant soft pretzels, and who was I to deny them? We made quick work of it, then got some ice cream to finish off the day. We ate it as we walked back to Theo's house. Shivers ran down my spine with the combination of the cold ice cream and the dropping temperature as the sun began to fall beneath the horizon. We watched the sunset as we walked, beautiful pinks and purples painting the sky.

Once we got in the door, Theo made a beeline for their room. I instead went to the guest room to rummage around my suitcase for some pajamas to change into. After changing, I made my way up the stairs into Theo's room, but they were nowhere to be found. I could hear the sink running in the bathroom, they must've been in there.

I'd planned on getting into bed and pulling up some show for us to watch while we cuddled, when an open notebook on Theo's desk caught my eye, the lamp illuminating the page, begging for it to be read.

Depression is more than a diagnosis

It's a life sentence

Responsibilities pile up
And suddenly
Those things you've taken for granted
Become impossible
Cleaning, eating, showering
Even sleep escapes you

That voice in your head
It feeds you lies
And tells you time and time again
How much better a place the world would be
Without you in it
Until you've heard it so many times
That you're not sure it's a lie anymore

You push it aside
People tell you chin up
Push though
It'll get better someday
Except it's been years
And better never seems to come

You'll have a day where it all seems okay
And then the very next you wish for death
You're reminded of every mistake
Every misstep

You're awful
You're useless
You'll never get it right
Except no one remembers but you
These insignificant blunders are the reason you deserve death

So you get high
You get drunk
Looking for anything to help you survive
The constant wave of pain that washes over you
You want that release
That relief
But it's only temporary

You start to let people down
And it only compounds
How horrible you feel
You try your best
And it's not enough
You'll never be enough
To match up to the ideal you in your head

That person is Good
That person is Strong
That person is Loved

And you don't feel like any of that

You punish yourself for not meeting expectations
You scream

You cry
You bang your head
You take blades to your skin
And wish it all to be over

Except you're scared
You don't know what's After
You don't even want to die
But you feel selfish for being alive
You feel like the only service you can do
Is to stop being here
Stop taking up space

The voice starts to scream
Everyone would be happier if you died
You should hurt yourself
You should end it
Do everyone the favor

You contemplate the pills easily within your grasp
And instead
Pick up the phone
Call a crisis center
Where you're referred to go to the hospital

You spend the next few years
In and out of treatment
It waxes and wanes
Some days you're better
You crawl

And you fight
Until the better days outnumber the worse

You're on a high
You're getting things done
You're accomplishing your dreams
Until you slip again

And depression is waiting for you
Hungry as ever

I jumped as the door creaked open, and quickly wiped a tear from my cheek, trying to hide it. It was no use, I'd been caught.

"Al, what's wro—" They stopped mid sentence as they saw my hand on the page of the notebook.

I was quick to explain myself, "I'm sorry I read it, it was open and the poem caught my eye. I should've just closed it, I didn't mean to—"

"Al, it's okay. I'm not mad."

I sighed audibly, running my hand over the page again. "Do you really feel like this?"

They walked next to me and closed the book lightly, siding it off the desk into a drawer. "Sometimes."

"Lately?"

"Yeah, kinda."

"You know it's not true, right? I wouldn't be happier if you were gone. I need you, right now especially."

They sat down on their bed, dropping their face into their hands. I sat down next to them and ran my hand through the back of their hair.

"Everything's just so *wrong*. You got kicked out of your house because of me."

"Theo, the only thing I miss about that house is my sister. It never felt like home for me. *You're* what I need. You're my home."

They sniffled a little and looked at me, striking golden eyes brimming with tears. "I love you."

"I love you too." I leaned my head onto theirs and they buried my face in the crook of their neck. We sat in silence for a few minutes.

"It's a beautiful poem, though." I broke the silence.

"You think so?"

"I do."

CHAPTER NINE

I woke up first on the sleepy Sunday morning after our mall trip. I rolled over and wrapped my arms around Theo's waist, pulling them close and burying my face in the back of their neck. The sun was barely peeking in through the window, rising slowly in the sky, still surrounded by the pink and orange of the sunrise. I was *never* up this early. I pulled Theo in tighter and closed my eyes, willing myself to go back to sleep. Instead, Theo stirred and turned around to face me, eyes squinted to try and see me without their glasses.

"Why are you up so early?" Their voice was groggy, still overtaken with sleep.

"I don't know, I just woke up. Sleeping has been hard lately."

They wrapped their arms around my back and pulled me in, kissing me on the forehead. I ran my hands down their back until my fingers brushed the hem of their tank top, then slid my fingers underneath to feel their warm skin. It was so soft, and I tilted my head down to kiss them on the lips. They followed my lead, sliding their hands beneath my shirt and sending electric pulses out from their fingertips. I kissed them deeply, inhaling their scent through my nose. I wanted to be so close to them, crack their chest open and crawl inside. To live in their embrace forever.

Their hands suddenly flew off me, and at first I was confused until Theo exclaimed, "Mom! You don't knock?"

I shot upwards to see Monica standing in the doorway, a look equal parts horror and amusement on her face. My face flushed red, and I fixed the strap of my tank top that Theo had slid down.

"I didn't think you'd be awake this early." There was a chuckle in her voice. "I was just checking in, I'm about to leave for a double so I won't be home until late. I trust you two are being safe?"

"Mom." Theo's voice was a growl.

"I'm serious. There's supplies in the bathroom, I know you're not exactly going to need condoms but—"

"Mom!" Theo's voice cracked as they shouted and threw a pillow towards the door.

Monica laughed, shaking her head and closing the door as she turned to leave.

I couldn't help it. I had the blanket pulled up over my face and started giggling into it. It must've sounded like sobs, because Theo's voice was laced with concern.

"It's okay, Al, she's just being a mom. She's not mad—oh, *oh*. You're laughing."

Theo pulled the blanket down to expose my bright red face and tears as my giggles turned into the most unattractive snorts.

They pushed my shoulder playfully. "You really think it's that funny?"

I nodded, unable to speak through the fits of laughter.

There was a knock at the door, Theo rolled their eyes. "Come in."

It was Monica again, "I almost forgot, Alex, you have that gyno appointment that I made for you tomorrow after school. I'll take you in, if you want Theo, there that's up to you."

My stomach dropped. I nodded and Monica closed the door softly behind her as she left. I'd forgotten all about my nonexistent periods and how there might be something wrong.

Theo brushed a strand of hair out of my face. "What's the matter?"

"T, what if there's something really wrong with me? My mom always told me it was normal for girls in my family, what if she was lying this whole time? She lied to me enough times, I don't know if I can trust what she said."

They kissed my forehead. "Let's not worry about it until we know what's going on. Do you want me to come?"

"If you wouldn't feel weird, yeah."

"Of course not, I'll be there for whatever you need."

"Okay." I lay back down and Theo followed, resting their head inches from my face. The mood had been sufficiently killed, but we weren't about to go back to sleep either.

"Talk to me about something else, my brain's getting all buzzy."

Theo's face broke into a smile. "Mom might let me get a dog."

Up until this point, they had said absolutely nothing about wanting a dog, so this was news to me. They bounced a little under the sheets, as if they couldn't contain the excitement.

"I didn't know you wanted one."

"I didn't really think about it until my therapist brought it up that one might do me some good. I could take it out for runs. She said if I get one with the right temperament it could be a good therapy dog, help with my anxiety. I love dogs."

I was incredibly down for this idea. "How do we convince Monica?"

"My therapist talked to her about it with me, she's already halfway there. She's just worried taking care of it will be too much stress for me. I keep telling her that it won't, I think I just gotta badger her a little more and she'll give in."

"What kind do you want?"

"I dunno, I think I'll just go see what they have at the shelter. I don't want anything that's too high energy, that might be too much for me. Something calm that'll snuggle but still be willing to go for runs."

"You're taking me when you go to the shelter."

"Obviously." They rolled their eyes at the idea of me not coming.

We lay there for a minute, faces inches away from one another. My eyes started to close, and I thought I might get a little more sleep, until a loud grumble came from my stomach.

"God damn it." I muttered.

Theo snickered. "Let's make banana pancakes."

They didn't cook much compared to their brother, but they knew how to make the basics. They could make some damn good pancakes and liked to throw in ingredients just to see what would stick. Before I even answered them, they were out of bed, throwing on a pair of joggers over their boxers. They pulled me from the bed, and I followed groggily after them, slowing down on the stairs so I didn't fall.

"Can we put chocolate in them too?"

"Way ahead of you." They'd already pulled a jar of Nutella along with the pancake mix from the pantry. I got a large bowl from the cupboard and Theo peeled a couple bananas and started mashing them. I got a pan out while Theo mixed the whole concoction together with a whisk, making a way bigger mess than was necessary. I spread some butter around in the pan, just in time for Theo to come over to the stove and dump some batter into it. They set the bowl on the counter, splattering batter all around.

"You're such a mess, you need your own clean-up crew." I snickered at them.

"At least it's a *tasty* mess," they quipped, running a finger along the counter to pick up the batter and then lick it.

Rolling my eyes, I got out a couple plates, then started cleaning the counters of the powdered pancake mix that Theo had gotten *everywhere*. By the time I finished cleaning, Theo already had three pancakes on each plate and enough batter left over to make even more. They turned off the stove and grabbed butter and syrup before bringing the plates over to the island in front of the stools. We sat down side by side, and I scraped off a pad of butter and poured some syrup on mine as Theo did the same to theirs. I cut off a piece and reveled in the chocolatey banana goodness that graced my mouth. Theo was a mess in the kitchen, but the results spoke for themselves, even if it was from the powdered mix.

As usual, I finished my plate long before Theo did. They'd been big pancakes, so for once I didn't go in for seconds. Instead, I turned to Theo after glancing at the bowl of batter left on the counter.

"Should we make some for Seth? He's always feeding us."

They nodded, mouth full of pancakes. "Go for it."

I pulled another plate from the cupboard and turned the stove back on, grabbing some more butter to grease the pan. Using up the rest of the batter, I made three really janky shaped pancakes for Seth. I could never get them to be perfect circles for some reason. I hoped he wouldn't care what they looked like, just that they tasted good. As I was about to put them into the fridge, Seth came down the stairs and looked over at us.

"You guys beat me to breakfast, huh?"

I smiled and held out the plate for him. "For you."

He grinned. He wasn't used to people making food for him,

so he took the plate gleefully. He didn't even comment on how messed up the pancakes looked.

Sitting down at the island and pouring some syrup over the pancakes, he asked, "What are you two up to today?"

Theo and I exchanged looks as I brought the dirty pan and bowl over to the sink to start washing.

"We don't know yet," Theo answered.

I fell into a meditative state washing the dishes and didn't hear anything else. I could wash dishes forever, it was so calming. My hands in the warm, soapy water. The noise the sponge made as it scraped against the pan. The iridescent sheen the bubbles had. It brought me to another world. One with fields of suds that you could frolic through and you could feel a warm breeze on your face. I went through the pan, the bowl, one plate, two plates, three… wait,

I'd only had my plate.

My attention snapped up and I realized Theo had been handing me dishes as I'd been washing. I smiled and kissed them lightly on the lips, drying my hands on a dish towel and hanging it back up on the stove. They led me up the stairs and closed the door quickly behind us, pressing me against it and kissing me in a way that said they wanted more.

My stomach grumbled and ached a little. "I don't feel great," I whispered when we paused for air.

They changed gears immediately, pulling me over to the bed and bundling me up in a blanket before slipping their joggers off and then settling into the bed themself, pulling me into their lap, stroking my hair. "What's wrong?"

"My stomach hurts, and I'm really tired. Will you just hold me?" I freed one arm from the blanket cocoon to wrap around their waist.

"Of course," they whispered.

____

The next school day was more of the same, except Theo made their return. We fought our way through the halls, and I struggled to pay attention, mind wandering to my appointment and what kind of news I might get that day. At least I had all my homework finished this time, and the teachers didn't seem to notice how absentminded I was during classes.

It was time. Monica pulled up to the clinic and we walked inside, Theo holding my hand the whole way.

Monica approached the desk. "We have an appointment for Alexandra Kensington."

I winced a little, associating my full name with my mother's anger. The lady at the desk handed Monica a clipboard with some paperwork and we went and sat down in the waiting room. She showed me the papers.

"Fill out what you can, honey. It's okay if you don't know everything."

I took the clipboard from her and scanned over the papers. I paused at the gender question, grinning and tapping Theo's shoulder. "Look, there's a non-binary option!"

"Seriously?" They snatched the sheet, a smile gracing their face to match mine. "That's so cool." Laying an arm across my shoulders, they handed me back the clipboard and I went to work filling it out.

Before I was done, a woman called my name. I got up and followed her, Theo trailing behind me. Monica stayed back in the waiting room. The woman, who I assumed to be a nurse, led us through some winding hallways of exam rooms before stopping in front of a station.

"We're just going to take some vitals on you."

I nodded, handing the clipboard to Theo to hold as the nurse took my blood pressure, weight, and pulse. Then, the nurse led us to an exam room and gestured for us to sit down. I sat on the exam table, paper crinkling as I moved. Theo sat in a small chair in the corner. The nurse handed me a gown.

"Please change into this, and the doctor will be right with you." The nurse smiled as she left.

Theo turned around to face the corner and covered their eyes. I snickered at them.

"It's not like you haven't seen me naked before."

"I know, but it feels weird now. I'm just gonna let you change."

I rolled my eyes, pulling my shoes and socks off before unbuttoning my pants and pulling my shirt over my head. I put the gown on and tied the strings. "Okay, you can look now."

They turned around just as we heard a knock on the door.

"Come in," I said, sitting back down on the exam table.

The doctor who walked in was a small brunette woman with a few visible tattoos on her arms. It occurred to me that I'd never seen a doctor with tattoos before. I thought it was pretty cool. She had a calming air about her that instantly put me at ease and I relaxed my posture a little.

"Alexandra?" she asked.

"Alex," I nodded.

"Okay, Alex. I'm Dr. Sherwin. Is this your first time at a gynecologist? And who's this?" She glanced over at Theo briefly.

"Yeah, and that's Theo, my partner. I want them here if that's okay."

She nodded. "Okay, I've got a few questions before we begin."

She set the laptop she'd been holding on the counter and pulled up the vacant stool. "Do you have the papers the front desk gave you? I can get a lot of the information from there."

Theo handed Dr. Sherwin the clipboard and she set to typing. After a couple minutes, she looked up at me. "Alex, when was your last period?"

I glanced down at the floor, "That's kinda why I'm here. I've never had one."

Dr. Sherwin's eyebrows raised slightly. "And you're sixteen? Hm."

Not very reassuring.

"Are you sexually active?"

"I—uh… yes? Kind of?"

She raised an eyebrow at me, then looked at Theo's reddening face and nodded. "I see. Any chance you could be pregnant?"

"Don't you have to get your period first in order to get pregnant?"

"Not necessarily, there's all kinds of flukes that happen."

"I… I still don't think so. I haven't done anything with anyone other than Theo in months."

The doctor nodded, "Now, before I start with the exam, have you been having any other symptoms other than not getting your period?"

"No."

"All right, lie back on the table for me."

I lay down and she started a typical checkup, listening to my breathing, feeling my stomach, the whole deal. She then handed me a blanket to put over my lap.

"Theo, why don't you come stand at her head? I'm about to do the internal exam."

Theo got up and stood by my side, holding my hand as the doctor pulled an extension out of the table and had me put my feet on it, like the stirrups when people give birth.

"This might be a little uncomfortable, especially since you've never had this done. If you need to, you can wiggle your toes. It helps."

I glanced up at Theo who gave me a weak smile, then I took a deep breath as Dr. Sherwin pulled up the stool and sat in front of my legs, then started feeling around inside me. Tears brimmed in the corners of my eyes, and I started wiggling my toes almost immediately.

Theo rubbed my hand. "Breathe, baby."

I sucked in a deep breath, and only after focusing on my breathing for a few seconds did I notice the look on Dr. Sherwin's face. She was squinting, like something wasn't as it should be. She cocked her head sideways and felt deeper, making me whimper.

"Sorry, sweetie, I'm just having trouble finding your cervix."

I wasn't even sure what a cervix was. She felt around a little longer, then gave up, pulling her gloves off.

"If you don't mind, I'm going to try an ultrasound on you. I'll be right back with the equipment."

I let out a breath I'd been holding for half the exam, then wiped the tears from my eyes, sniffling a little. Putting my legs down on the table, I sat up and clung to Theo as they wrapped their arms around me.

"There's something really wrong with me, I know it."

"Let's just see what the ultrasound shows, okay? It might be nothing."

Dr. Sherwin returned a minute later with a monitor and an ultrasound machine. She had me pull up the gown with the blanket still over my legs to expose my stomach.

"This might be a little cold," she mentioned as she squirted a thick goo onto my stomach. I flinched a little, but it wasn't anywhere near as bad as the previous exam. She clicked on the monitor and started moving the wand around on my stomach. She squinted as she looked around. She was quiet. Really quiet.

"Um…" She stopped before she really said anything.

"What's wrong?" I fidgeted with my hands and Theo squeezed my arm.

"It's just… hold on. I'm going to get one of my colleagues' opinions first."

She left again, and I started to shake. "Can I worry now, Theo?" My tone was sharp and a little more sarcastic than I'd meant for it to be. I didn't mean to take anything out on them. I looked up to see a look of terror on their face that they tried to hide from me. They were afraid too.

"Yes," they whispered, "We can worry now."

It felt like forever before Dr. Sherwin returned, a much older doctor with graying hair coming in behind her. This doctor picked up the ultrasound wand and looked around for a few minutes, then looked back at Dr. Sherwin warily. She got up, nodded at Dr.Sherwin, then placed her hand briefly on her shoulder before walking out the door without saying a single word. That made me even more nervous.

Dr. Sherwin came and sat in the stool next to me, handing me tissues to clean the now-warm gel off my stomach. "It seems like you have a bit more going on than missed periods. It's apparent why you haven't had them." She turned the computer screen that had a few frozen pictures on it so that Theo and I could see. We didn't know what we were looking at.

She pulled up one that just looked like empty space to my untrained eye. "That's where your uterus should be."

"*Should* be?"

She nodded and pulled up another picture, pointing to a couple round masses. "And these aren't ovaries. They're testes."

I shot straight up on the table. "I have *testes?* I was born a boy?"

"Not exactly. In the community it's known as being intersex. You likely have Androgen Insensitivity Syndrome. It makes your body immune to testosterone. You probably have XY chromosomes, but developed seemingly as a girl because your body only accepts estrogen. Your gender identity doesn't change with this diagnosis, you just don't have the same equipment we assumed you did."

"Wait, wait, *wait.*" My brain slowly churned to try and process what she'd said. If I didn't have a uterus… "Can I have kids?"

"There's no uterus for you to carry one. You don't have eggs. So, I'm afraid not."

My stomach dropped through the floor, and I couldn't hold back the flood of tears that overcame me. I started sobbing, and Theo held me. I'd always wanted kids. I'd always wanted, when I was ready, to carry my own child to term and give birth. Now that possibility was ripped away from me, and I didn't know what to do with myself. Everything was wrong, so wrong. Was I even a girl? I mean, of course I was. I'd never questioned my gender identity. I was every bit a girl as Theo was agender. But this news made me question some things, everything. I couldn't breathe, my head was spinning, I was spiraling.

Theo rubbed my back, trying to calm me down. I was inconsolable. The doctor sat there patiently, waiting for me to come around. I wasn't sure I ever would.

CHAPTER TEN

I hadn't said a word since the doctor told me I couldn't have kids. I'd eventually stopped crying, but I couldn't hear anything other than a ringing in my ears as the doctor tried to explain everything about the syndrome she'd diagnosed me with. I wasn't there, it was as if a bomb had gone off right next to me and I was in shock. I didn't say anything as the doctor led us back out to the waiting room where Monica was. Nothing on the ride home. Nothing as I went straight up the stairs to Theo's room and buried myself in the blankets, silent tears falling the whole time. I think Monica had tried to ask me what happened, but I didn't even register it. I was gone. Numb.

Theo came up to their room and sat on the edge of the bed, brushing my hair out of my face and stroking my wet cheek. "Do you want to get high?" they asked so casually, like it was a natural response to your life as you'd imagined it ending.

"You mean weed, right?" I asked, muffled by the blankets.

They nodded, "I'd never offer you anything else, I'd never want you to go through the same addiction as me."

"Okay." The tears were starting to make the blanket damp.

I sat up as Theo dug through their bottom drawer and pulled out the familiar shoebox. They came and sat on the edge of the bed, making quick work of preparing a joint. I opened the window slightly to let the smoke out as Theo lit it up, taking a puff and exhaling the smoke. They handed it to me, and I tried to remember what I'd learned from the first time. I took in a small breath and managed to hold it for a couple seconds before coughing it out. Still not as graceful as Theo, but getting better. They took the joint and put the box back in their drawer, exhaling smoke as they walked back over to the bed and handed it back to me. I took a bigger hit and managed to only cough a little as I exhaled the smoke.

Theo pulled me into their lap as I handed them back the joint. I wrapped my arms around their thighs and sniffled a little. The tears had stopped, but my face was still wet and gross. They pulled a tissue from one of their shelves and handed it to me, I wiped my face and blew my nose, dropping the tissue on the floor.

"Do you want to talk about it?" They asked, blowing smoke out the window and handing me the joint one last time.

"No." I took a drag, then exhaled. "Not yet."

The room started warping a little bit in my vision, like it was slowly moving around me. Maybe I'd had too much. I clung to Theo as they finished off the joint, stubbing it out in a tissue and dropping it in the trash can. Closing my eyes against the movement around me, I still felt like a ship at sea. Moving ever so slightly, with a rhythm all my own. Closing my eyes might've actually made it worse. I opened my eyes and tried to focus on one spot in the room – Theo's desk chair. It was still, but everything around it slowly started to warp and I felt a buzzing in my ears. Anxiety rose up in me as I struggled to stay grounded.

"What happens if you have too much?" I managed to ask.

"It's different for different people, why? Are you okay?"

"I feel like everything's moving around me. Like I'm seasick."

"Mm. Yeah, that last hit might've been too much. Hold my hand."

They opened their palm for me to take and squeezed hard. The sensation brought me back down to earth a little, and I took in a deep breath.

"You're okay," they cooed, "It'll pass. Nothing's going to happen to you here."

I continued to focus on the pressure of their hand holding mine and the deep breaths I tried to take. At some point, I must've fallen asleep, because then everything went blank.

———

I awoke with a start the next morning, panicking as I saw the clock read 9:07 AM. I flew out of bed and looked back to see Theo asleep as well.

"Theo, Theo!" I shook them and they jumped up.

"What's wrong?"

"Look at what time it is! Fuck, they're gonna call my mom!"

They squinted at the clock, then back at me. "Al, relax. Mom called them. I told her what happened with the doctor. She called the school and told them we're both sick, that you caught it from me."

The tension in my shoulders dropped, and I all but collapsed to the floor. The release sent tears falling from my eyes. God, I'd been crying so much lately, it felt pathetic. Theo got out of bed and wrapped their arms around me. I buried my face in the crook of their neck as the tears came out of me.

"Come back to bed," they whispered in my ear, sending tingles down my spine.

I followed as they guided me back towards the bed and wrapped me up.

"Today's gonna be about taking care of you, okay? You need it. All this is too much for anyone." They started walking towards the door after getting me situated in the bed.

"Where are you going?"

"To make you a nice bath. I have one of those fancy bath bombs that smell really nice. We're gonna have tea and watch a movie in a hot bath."

I nodded, staring down at my still emerald-green nails, remembering how relaxed I'd felt until yesterday. Why did everything good have to come to such an abrupt end lately? I just wanted some peace.

Theo left the room for a few minutes, and I could hear them moving about the house. I leaned back against the wall, closing my eyes, willing myself to go back to sleep. It had been such a dead sleep after getting too high, it felt like I'd blinked and then it was morning. My senses started to dull, and I started to drift off again, then it all came back in an instant as Theo opened the door.

My eyes flew open, and they came over to the bed and kissed me softly on the lips before running their hands down my arms and pulling me from the cocoon of blankets. I wobbled on my feet a little, head still full of sleep. They led me to the bathroom, and I was overcome with sweet scents of vanilla and lavender. Theo had lit a few vanilla candles, and the bath water was tinted purple, presumably with a lavender bath bomb. It was warm and steamy, I hardly noticed as Theo pulled the hoodie over my head and off of me. They stripped off their own clothing as I took off my sports bra and underwear, and they pulled the small stool they'd taken from their room up to the edge of the bath and opened their laptop to a movie.

They stepped into the water and held out a hand for me to follow. The sensation of heat tingled against my legs, penetrating my skin and making me feel warm down to the bone. Theo sat down and pulled me up against them as I took a deep breath of lavender with my nose inches from the water. They hit play on their laptop and then we were in another world. One where none of the bad stuff could touch us, one where we were safe from bullies and our bodies betraying us.

We stayed in the bath until it went cold and the movie was long over. Once I started shivering, Theo made the move to get out. I still didn't want to, I wanted to stay hidden in this world of lavender and vanilla forever, but without their body heat buffering me against the cold water I was forced to get out. They wrapped me in the fluffiest towel I'd ever felt, blew out the candles, and removed the plug for the bath to drain. I stood there shivering in the towel, probably looking like a drowned rat with running mascara from the makeup I'd forgotten to take off. Unless I'd already cried it all off, which was likely.

Theo wrapped their own towel around themself and tucked the end in so that it would stay without them holding it, then picked up the stool and their laptop. The rush of cold air smacked me in the face as they opened the door and made me shiver even more as we made the short, two-foot trek back to their room. Once we were inside, Theo closed the door and dug through their dresser, pulling out an oversized hoodie and a pair of boxers and handed them to me. I eagerly embraced the hoodie, dropping the towel and pulling my still damp hair through the head hole. I slipped the boxers on, which were completely concealed by how long the hoodie was. This thing must've gone down past Theo's knees – I was six inches taller than them – why did they even have this? In the moment, I was grateful that they did as I threw myself back into the bed and Theo dug out clothes for themself.

After they were dressed, they asked, "What kind of pizza do you want? Mom left me some money."

Pizza sounded *so good.* "Spinach and feta," I said into the pillow, looking up in time to see Theo wrinkle their nose.

"Eugh, seriously? I hate spinach on pizza."

I dropped my face back into the pillow, "Mushroom and feta then."

"That's better," they snickered.

They ordered the pizza, then sat on the edge of the bed, running their hands through my wet hair, then grabbing a towel to try and dry it off a little more. I heard them get up, then they returned a couple minutes later to run what felt like a comb through my hair. They made their way through the wet and tangled mess, and I sighed. Having them do my hair was always relaxing. They were so gentle, never yanking the strands or pulling at my tender head. After they finished combing it, they pulled everything back into a French braid.

The doorbell rang just as they finished, and they went downstairs to retrieve the pizza. They came back up with the warm box in hand and I sat up immediately, ready to dig in. Theo placed the box on my lap as they picked up the hair products off the bed and set them on their desk. I had opened the box and put a slice in my mouth before they sat down next to me, taking their own piece.

"Is there anything you want to do?" they asked after swallowing a mouthful of pizza.

"Disappear," I muttered.

They leaned over and kissed me, leaving a bit of grease on my cheek that I wiped off with the sleeve of the hoodie.

"I know the feeling," they said, trying to offer me some empathy.

"I just. I always wanted to have a kid. Ever since I was a little girl, I wanted to be a mom when I got older."

"You can still be a mom."

I glanced at them, feeling insensitive to their experience, not sure how to say what was in my head without insulting their adoption. "I know, I just…"

"…wanted a kid that was actually yours?"

"No, that's not… what I mean. Monica is really your mom, I know that, I'm not—"

"Al, it's okay. I get it, it's a huge disappointment. It's something you've always wanted that was suddenly taken away from you."

"I wanted a baby. I wanted to have my own baby." I whispered, tears silently beginning to fall.

Theo put an arm around my shoulders, pulling me closer as I continued to stuff my face with pizza. Emotional eating at its finest.

A thought rushed through my head, and I sat up so fast I almost dropped the whole pizza box. "Do you think my mom knew? What if she knew this entire time and just didn't tell me? She did brush off the thing about my periods, telling me girls in the family get them late. What if she was making up excuses? What if she *knew?*"

"Al, slow down. I don't know if your mom knew, but what does it matter now? It's not like anything could've been prevented."

"It would mean she lied to me my entire life! She let me think my whole life that I was a normal girl, but I'm… what did the doctor call it?"

"Intersex."

I'm glad they'd been level-headed enough to retain the information.

"You're still a girl, Alex. You're like the most girl person I've ever met."

"I know, it just… feels different now. Everything feels different. I want to talk to my mom. I want to know if she knew."

"Are you sure that's a good idea? She threatened to send you to a conversion camp, I don't want her to have the chance to do that to you."

"What if you came with me?"

"That actually might be an even worse idea."

I doubled back on my thinking. They were right. "What if Monica came with me?"

Theo tilted their head to the side, squinting a bit. "That's a better idea."

I sighed, leaning my head on Theo's shoulder. Over the course of the conversation, I'd made my way through two and a half pieces of pizza. My stomach wanted me to stop, but my brain and mouth wanted me to keep going. I took another bite.

CHAPTER ELEVEN

The rest of the day flew by, Elliot and Harriet both texting me with concern. Jeremy texted Theo, asking to come over because his mom was in another stupor. So while I lay in bed trying to plan out a meeting with my mother, Theo tidied up their room, hiding the evidence that we'd decided to smoke after our bath. I had a lot less this time and the room wasn't spinning. Just enough for my eyes to squint a little with a soft buzz in my head. It didn't take away all the stress, but it dulled it just enough to be tolerable. I'd ended up eating half the pizza afterwards though.

We heard sounds downstairs, presumably Seth and Jeremy getting home and settling in. There was a knock at the door just as Theo tied the trash bag containing the butt end of the joint (which Theo had explained to me was called a roach, as I'd been completely confused when they said they were looking for a roach in the trash) and the tissue we'd stubbed it out in.

"Come in."

Jeremy poked his head in the door, took one whiff and said, "You guys smoking? I want some."

Theo playfully pushed Jeremy's shoulder. "Get outta here, you can seriously smell it? We blew the smoke out the window and I sprayed air freshener."

He laughed while trying to hide a wince. "Yeah, I know that's the air freshener you use to cover up the weed, you've done it enough times with me here."

They rolled their eyes. "We finished off the joint, I'll roll another one later and you can have some."

"Damn," he muttered, dropping his bag next to the desk and plopping into the desk chair. He caught sight of me under the covers. "How're you doing, Alex?"

"Shitty," I muttered mindlessly, still in the world of my thoughts. I looked at him for a brief moment, trying to focus my eyes and noticed a bit of purple peeking out from his t-shirt. "Are the assholes at school on you, or did your mom do that?"

He glanced briefly at his arm and then pulled down his sleeve, but Theo was having none of that. As soon as I pointed it out Theo went over to him and pulled up the sleeve, revealing a bruise that took up most of his bicep.

"Mom…" he said under his breath.

Theo disappeared from the room and returned a minute later with a tube of some type of cream, then lifted up Jeremy's sleeve again. Jeremy tried to pull away and Theo lightly smacked him on the back of his head.

"Hold still, loser, this'll help."

Jeremy resigned to his fate as Theo rubbed the cream into the bruise on his shoulder. They finished soon enough and then set the tube down on the desk and let Jeremy pull his sleeve back down.

"When did she do that?" Theo came and sat on the edge of the bed, keeping eye contact with Jeremy.

"This morning. I missed the bus and didn't realize she was already drunk when I asked to take the car. Ended up walking to school."

"You're on the other side of town!"

"I know, I missed my first class, I'm sure they called her about it and she's pissed about that too. I didn't want to go home and find out."

"You can stay the night if you want, Al doesn't sleep in the guest room anyway." Theo put a hand on Jeremy's non-bruised shoulder.

"Thanks, yeah, I think I'll stay here tonight. The anniversary of my dad dying is tomorrow. I know she'll be even worse then."

"Shit, I'm sorry, Jer."

"I feel bad, not being there for her. But she takes it all out on me."

"Don't feel bad about not wanting to get hit. We all have grief, it's not an excuse to hurt someone."

Jeremy nodded, taking in a deep breath. "If he was still here, she wouldn't be like this. I wish I was enough to pull her out of it."

"You should be, it's her own fault for not seeing that. You're not there to be her punching bag."

"It's hard not to let it get to me. I feel like a terrible son."

"It's her that's being terrible, Jer. You're just trying to survive."

Jeremy sniffed a little, staring down at the floor as the wheels in his brain visibly started turning.

"Oh, roll him a joint, Theo."

Theo rolled their eyes at me. "Fine, but you're not having more now. I don't want you getting weird again." They walked over to their dresser and pulled out the shoebox.

"When did you start smoking anyway, Alex? You've always been miss vanilla." Jeremy came out from his thoughts long enough to taunt me.

"Since everything sucks. Guess what, I'm not even a girl!" I sat up, waving my arms about as I spoke.

Theo stiffened a little. They still had their back turned to me, but I could tell what I said irritated them. "You're still a girl, Alex."

I was too caught up in my own spiraling thought process to consider Theo's feelings this time.

Jeremy cocked his head at me, "What?"

"I'm intersex. Can't have babies. I have freaking testes! No kids for me!"

He squinted at me, like he couldn't process what I'd said. "Wouldn't you have, like, noticed that?"

"Nope! They're all up inside me *pretending* to be ovaries." I smacked my stomach with both hands, the thick hoodie I was wearing absorbing the blow. "I'm a fucking freak of nature."

Theo got up, wordlessly handing Jeremy a joint and a lighter, then walked out of the room. I'd gone too far.

Jeremy glanced between the door and me, holding the joint like it had just smacked him in the face. Tears started streaming down my face and my lip quivered as I tried to hold back the flood that threatened to overtake me. I watched Jeremy as he set the joint on the desk, then left the room to go after Theo, closing the door behind him. Getting up, I pressed my ear to the door, trying to hear the hallway conversation. It wasn't too hard, they were just outside the door. I could hear Theo pacing while Jeremy tried to be the voice of reason.

"If she thinks she's a freak, what does that make me? I'm the one who's actually not a girl."

"C'mon, Theo, you know she doesn't mean that. She's just upset. It's big news to have sprung on you."

Theo got a lot quieter, and their voice cracked. "I can't fix this for her, Jer."

"She doesn't need you to fix it. She just needs time."

There was silence for a minute, then a shuffling and a turn to the door handle. I scrambled back into bed before the door opened, making a poor attempt to hide the fact that I'd been listening. I grabbed a tissue and tried to wipe the tears from my face.

"I'm sorry, T. I didn't mean anything by it."

Silently, they sat down next to me, and then brushed a lock of hair out of my face and behind my ear. "Don't ever call my girlfriend a freak again."

I tried to stop the smile that cracked across my lips. God damn, they were charming when they wanted to be. Leaning in, I kissed them. Jeremy lit the joint and then tapped Theo on the shoulder with it after taking a hit. Theo took it and pushed the window open again, blowing the smoke outside. Instinctively, I reached for it, but Theo pulled it away.

"Uh-uh, no more for you, remember?" They handed it back to Jeremy.

I crossed my arms like a pouting child. "I'm not even that high anymore."

They looked me up and down, then took the joint as Jeremy passed it back to them. "*One* hit."

I took it eagerly, ready for my head to feel light and floaty again. I wanted to escape. I took the biggest breath I could in, not caring about the consequences. The coughing started before I'd even finished inhaling.

"Aaaand that's enough." Theo took the joint out of my hand, taking another smooth drag that put me to shame.

Jeremy laughed, "Still don't quite have it down, do you?"

"Shut up," I said through my fit of coughing.

There was a knock on the door and Theo quickly hid the joint behind their back as the door opened. They sighed with relief as

Seth poked his head in the door. "Can I get a hit?"

"Shit, can you smell it?"

"Nah." He opened the door more and walked in, shutting it behind him, "But I can hear Alex coughing from the bottom of the stairs."

They all looked at me as little puffs of smoke came out each time I coughed. Theo handed Seth what was left of the joint, and he finished it off. They all put me to shame, these smooth smokers, making it look easy. My face felt hot, and I imagined it was bright red.

Seth patted me on the back. "You'll get the hang of it."

I rolled my eyes as he walked to the door.

"Later," he said, closing the door behind him.

Theo reopened the bag from earlier and stubbed the new roach out in the same tissue as the other one. They tied up the bag and left the room with it, presumably to go bury it in the outside trash. I flopped back on the bed, staring at the ceiling as Jeremy sprayed some more of the air freshener. Afterwards, he sat back down in the desk chair.

"Testes, huh?"

"Two of them."

————

Hours later, I made my way down the stairs with still-squinted eyes, hoping Monica wouldn't notice. I needed this talk with my mother to happen, and I needed her help to do it.

She was in the kitchen, making a cup of tea. She had let her curly blond hair down, the ends barely meeting her shoulders. The scrubs she was wearing meant she'd just gotten in the door. I felt bad springing this on her right after she got home, but it was now or never.

I approached her. She still had her back turned as I softly asked, "Monica?"

She jumped a little, almost spilling her tea as she turned to look at me.

"Sorry," I muttered.

She let out a sigh. "No, it's alright kiddo, I just had a bit of a rough shift. What's up?"

"I wanted to talk about what happened about the appointment, if that's okay." I awkwardly shuffled my weight between my feet, unable to stand still.

"Sure. Why don't I make you a cup of tea as well, then we can sit and talk?"

"Okay." I didn't really want tea, but it felt bad to refuse. At least it would give my hands something to do while we were talking.

Monica pulled out another cup and a tea bag, added water, then stuck them in the microwave. After it beeped, she pulled it out and put some honey in, stirring it with a spoon. She handed me the cup, and then we both went to the living room, her sitting in an oversized armchair and me sinking into the couch.

"How much did Theo tell you?"

"Just that you learned you couldn't have kids and were really upset by it, that you needed some time."

"The lady said I have…" I squinted, trying to remember what she'd said, "Androgen… something syndrome."

"Androgen Insensitivity Syndrome?"

"Yeah, that. She said it means I'm intersex."

Monica nodded.

"Is that rare?"

"Androgen Insensitivity Syndrome itself is on the rare side, yes.

But being intersex is a lot more common than people think, around one in every hundred. There's a lot of different ways someone can be intersex."

"Would my mom have known about it, do you think?"

"I don't know, hun. It all depends on how you presented as a baby. People with Complete Androgen Insensitivity don't always show many symptoms, until they're old enough to get their period and don't. So if you have the Complete version, it's likely she didn't know. Some people don't even find out until they get a check-up when trying to have kids."

"So it's possible she could've known, though?"

"It's possible, yes."

"Do… do you think you could come with me to talk to her? I need to know if she knew."

"Hun, I'm not sure if that's a good idea, especially with how she came over here after you left home."

"That's why I want you to come. You can get me out of there if I need you to. I just really need to talk to her. I need to know if she kept this from me." I gripped the cup in my hands tighter.

She leaned forward in the chair, setting her tea down on the coffee table, then made eye contact with me again. "If you really need to, yes. I'll come with you."

I sighed, leaning back a little. "Thank you."

"Is there anything else you want to talk about? I'm sure you have questions."

Tears forced their way into my eyes, I tried to blink them back. "I really can't have kids?"

"No, honey. I'm sorry."

My lip quivered as I sat there in silence, again trying to force back the tears that threatened to overtake me. I stared into space as my ears started ringing just like they had in the doctor's office.

Monica cleared her throat. "You know, I couldn't have kids either."

That got my attention. "Really?"

She nodded. "I had endometriosis so bad that it affected my uterus, and I needed a hysterectomy in my mid-twenties to stop the pain. I was still in medical school, and hadn't even had time to think about kids. The pain was so debilitating that I didn't second-guess the decision until my early thirties when I realized how badly I wanted a child."

"So you had a choice?"

"In a way, yes, but also no. The pain would've ruined my life. it left me bedbound. Because of that surgery, I was able to complete medical school and get where I am now. I still have two beautiful children, so it all worked out in the end."

"Wasn't it hard, connecting with a kid when you weren't there from the very beginning? Not being able to talk to them before they were even born? I mean, I know you love Seth and Theo, and they needed you, but I just… I really wanted to carry a child."

"Getting pregnant is a unique experience, for sure, but it's not what makes you bond with your child. As soon as you think of a child as yours, that's when the love starts. Even if they weren't always yours, once they are there's no turning back."

"Seth doesn't even call you 'mom' though."

"That's a piece I had to let go. He won't call me that because he had and still remembers a mother that wasn't me, and he feels like calling me 'mom' would be disrespectful to her, rest her soul. I understand why he does it, and I've learned to live with it. I'll tell you though, there was nothing like the first time Theo called me 'mom'."

"You missed all the baby years though, so many firsts."

"But you don't have to. There's plenty of ways to start with a baby. And besides, there's always more firsts to be had. Honey, this isn't the end of a dream. It's just an adjustment to it. In a way, taking in a child that wouldn't have a home otherwise is even more rewarding. In some ways it's more work, and you have to make up for mistakes you didn't make, but getting to where I am with Theo and Seth is a journey I wouldn't trade for anything."

"What about all the pain they have, doesn't it hurt you too?"

"Of course it does, but if you were willing to undergo childbirth, pain doesn't scare you."

I nodded, finally taking a sip of my now lukewarm tea.

Monica smiled and placed a hand on my knee, "You'll be okay, sweetheart, you really will. It's okay to be upset about it, but it's not the end of your world."

"Thank you." I placed my tea down on the table and wrapped my arms around myself. "I feel a little better."

"Glad I could help, is there anything else?"

"What do I say to my mom?"

CHAPTER TWELVE

Monica and I walked up to the familiar door just a couple streets over from the home that had shown me so much safety. She stood behind me, and my hand shook as I knocked on the door, chipping paint falling off as I struck it with my knuckles.

The door opened and it was like all the breath was sucked from my body. My mother's expression went from one of greeting to a scowl the minute she saw me. Then, I swear there were tears behind her eyes.

"Have you come to your senses? Will you go to the camp if I arrange it?"

"Absolutely not." Monica's tone was sharp behind me.

"Then why are you here?"

All the words I'd played over and over in my head were gone, and I was grasping at whatever I could find to try and have this conversation. This was so much harder face to face, rather than imagining her in front of me. Her mere presence threw me off balance as I searched for the words that had been right there a second ago.

Before I could get anything out, the padding of quick

footsteps behind my mom caught me off guard. Before my mom could stop her, Leah was on the doorstep with her arms wrapped around my waist.

I knelt down to hug her. "Hi, baby." I knew she couldn't hear me, but she'd feel the vibrations of me speaking and that had always soothed her.

After a minute, I noticed how tightly she was clinging, and she wouldn't let go. My mom bent down and pried her off of me, and then signed "Go to your room." Tears started falling down Leah's cheeks and she stamped her foot.

She actually yelled, "No!"

My mom's posture stiffened even more and her eyebrows slanted in anger. She pointed firmly in the direction of Leah's room.

Leah's signing was frantic. "You made her leave, I want her back! You can't make her go away again!"

My mom was shaking in anger, a sight that was familiar to me, but not Leah. I'd never seen her get angry like this at Leah, and out of fear for her I knelt down and placed a hand gently on Leah's shoulder to get her attention and signed, "It's okay, please go. I'll try and come see you soon."

Her tears fell hard and fast, and I placed a hand on the back of her head and kissed her on the forehead. She hung her head and reluctantly left, slumping her shoulders as she walked back to her room.

My mom's shaking anger hadn't dissipated, and her eyes were fire as she glared at me. "What do you want?"

"We need to talk." I glanced back at Monica for reassurance. I didn't want to go inside, but I also didn't want to have this conversation on the doorstep.

My mom didn't budge, but didn't shut the door either.

"I found out something's wrong with me, and I need to know if you knew." I couldn't look at her while I was speaking, but as soon as I was done, I studied her face to gauge her reaction.

Her face was stiff, no concern hiding anywhere. She didn't even care, I'd always known that I was the throwaway child to her. After a good minute of staring, she finally asked, "What's wrong?"

"I have Androgen Insensitivity Syndrome. You always told me people in the family just get periods late, but Monica took me to a doctor and they figured it out. Did you know?"

Her expression didn't change. There was another long silence, until she finally dropped the bomb. "Yes."

"Are you *serious?* You never thought to tell me? You just lied to cover it up?" I was furious, now it was me that was shaking with anger.

"It wasn't information you needed. I thought if I prayed enough, you'd turn out okay. I guess clearly I was wrong."

"*What?*" Wasn't information I needed? If she prayed enough I'd turn out okay? This was absolutely ridiculous, this was—"Is that why you never loved me as much as Leah?" My eyes narrowed, daring her to deny it.

"You were my trial. I had to show God that I could handle you properly."

"*Handle* me?" My thoughts were racing, I couldn't do anything but repeat her words in outrage.

"Yes, I thought with the surgery, everything would be okay. But you were always so defiant."

I was about to argue some more, but then the beginning of her sentence hit me. "What surgery?"

"The one to fix you, when you were a baby. Your privates were messed up."

I'd read about it in the obsessive research I'd done after my conversation with Monica. I wanted to know everything there was to know about my syndrome. Some people with it are born with ambiguous genitals. Sometimes the doctors tell the parents to choose and then have a surgery for the baby to "fix" them, even though the surgery wasn't medically necessary. The intersex community as a whole had spoken out largely against it and referred to it as genital mutilation.

Unnecessary, essentially cosmetic, invasive surgery, on *babies*. Surgery that the child might decide against once they were old enough for the decision.

And they'd done it to me.

I slammed the door shut in my mom's face.

———

When I got back to Theo's house, I lost it, in front of Monica, in front of whoever was home that I didn't even register as the sobs overcame me. Monica pulled me into a hug, and I buried my face in her chest.

Theo was down the stairs in an instant. They'd known where I was going and what I was doing. They must've been prepared for this. They pulled me from Monica's arms and took me into their own, kissing me as I nestled my face in the crook of their neck.

I felt so wrong. So violated. My mother knew the whole time, even approved an unnecessary surgery on me to make me how she thought I should be. I wasn't born like this, I was forced into this box, parts of me were literally cut to make me fit. I knew I wasn't what my mother wanted all along, I just didn't know how deep it went. I'd never been what she wanted, even as a baby. She'd prayed for something different. For so long, I'd tried to make her happy, not knowing that my very body defied her. It had all been useless,

I never could've lived up to her standards.

Theo guided me up to their room, and I collapsed onto the bed in a mess of tears. They sat down next to me, rubbing my back and cooing to me, trying to get me to calm down. How could I when it felt like such a huge part of my life had been nothing but lies? I started coughing, choking on my own saliva, Theo rolled me onto my side, brushing the hair out of my face.

"Breathe, baby, you've gotta breathe."

I couldn't. Breathing got away from me as I coughed harder, my face flushing red as tears and snot took over my face. I was a mess.

Theo grabbed a tissue and wiped my face, then laid down to face me, placing their hands on my cheeks. "Breathe with me, in… one… two… three…four…"

I tried hard to follow their direction, taking in a ragged breath that threatened to run out of me as I tried to trap it in my lungs. I managed to hold it for a second before Theo had me exhale for a count of eight, then again.

Eventually, I got it under control. My breathing calmed and the tears fell silently instead of with heavy sobs.

Theo rested their hand on the back of my head, stroking my hair. "Do you want to talk about it?"

Fuck talking. Talking had only gotten me hurt so far today. I didn't want to tell Theo what I'd learned from my mother, I was… ashamed. That my body was so wrong that doctors and my mom decided to change it without my consent. I was devastated, that I was now a statistic on the list of intersex people wronged by doctors.

The silence must've been uncomfortable for Theo. They squirmed a little. "It's okay if you don't. No pressure."

I focused on their face, their upturned eyebrows, golden eyes peering at me with concern. The freckles that embellished their cheeks, their full lips, the cute nose that I wanted to nuzzle.

I didn't want to talk. I wanted something else.

I ran my hands through their hair and pulled them closer to me, kissing them with intention. They kissed me back, and I wrapped my arms around their back, pulling up on their tank top.

They stopped, holding me at arms' length. "Wait, you were just so upset, are you serious?"

"Please." My voice was desperate, tears threatening to spill out of my eyes again, "I need this."

They got up, and the tears started streaming down my face again, until I realized they were locking the door. Coming back, they sat down on the bed next to me, wiping the tears from my face as my whole body shook. They pulled me into their lap and held me close, placing their hands underneath my shirt at the small of my back. It sent shivers down my spine as I rested my arms on their shoulders, losing myself in the sensations.

This was how I'd always used sex. It was my coping mechanism. It's why I'd bounced so easily between guys before I was with Theo. The person meant nothing to me at the time, they were just a means to an end. I wanted the release, to lose myself in the feelings and tactile sensations of it. It was enough to distract me from whatever I was dealing with, if only for a minute.

I had an addiction, and it wasn't drugs.

I'd never used Theo like this before, and I was sure I'd feel bad about it later. In the moment, it was what I craved. I needed something to take me away from this world, something to distract me from the storm raging in my head. And Theo did such a good job of it, they always made me feel cared for, loved, wanted. Perfect as I was. I needed the feeling so badly that I ignored their shaking, their shallow breathing. Their obvious warning signs that I was usually attuned to. I didn't tell them it was okay to stop, like I usually did. I didn't tell them that they were safe, that nothing could hurt them here. I let them push themself until they broke.

But they didn't break outwardly, no. They were trying to make me feel better, so they held the pain inside. They hid their emotions like they'd been trained to do for so much of their life, and they hid them well. Well enough that they were easy for me to ignore in the moment, until we were done.

I lay back down, taking in deep breaths and staring up at the ceiling as Theo stumbled out of bed, desperate to get out. They threw on a bathrobe and left the room, then I heard the bathroom door shut. I let myself float there in the silence, still on the high of what we'd just done, still pushing the concern for Theo out of my mind. I'd detached myself from the moment. I let the tingling sensations in my body take me to another place, feeling as though I was on a cloud. The high that I got from this let me escape.

And then I heard a muffled sob come from the next room over. I couldn't ignore it anymore, and the consequences of what I'd just let happen came crashing down around me. I'd let them get triggered, didn't leave them with a way out. They'd felt trapped in the situation, or wanted too badly to make me feel better, something along those lines. They felt like they had to do it, so they pushed themself past their breaking point.

I threw on an oversized hoodie and some shorts, then knocked lightly on the bathroom door. "T?" It was almost a whisper. I was so wracked with guilt over what I'd just done.

There was no answer, but they'd forgotten to lock the door, so I opened it and locked it behind me. The shower was running with the curtain drawn, scalding hot water steaming up the whole room.

I pulled back the curtain to see Theo curled up under the water, shaking as they hugged their knees to their chest. Stripping off my clothes, I sat down behind them, gently placing my hands on their shoulders. They jumped, a sob escaping them as their head shot upwards to see me.

"I—I'm sorry, I wanted to make you feel better, I…" They shook their head, burying their face in their knees.

I pulled them so that they were leaning against me, "No, I'm sorry. I shouldn't have let you do that. It was too much."

They leaned into my shoulder, trying to get the sobs to stop. My skin was turning red from how hot the water was. How could they stand this? It was pouring down right on their face, masking their tears.

I kissed their forehead. "Can I turn the water down a little?"

They nodded, and I tipped the temperature just enough to take the edge off the sting of heat. We sat there under the water for a while, and Theo took their hand in mine.

"I guess we're both pretty fucked up, huh?" they muttered.

I couldn't stop the hollow laugh that came out of me. More than they knew. I had to tell them now, in the safety of the running water where no one else would hear.

"My mom did something really bad to me."

Theo lifted their head, looking me up and down. "Did she hurt you again? Monica was there! Nothing was supposed to happen!" The panic rose in their voice.

"No, she didn't do it while I was there with Monica. She did it a long time ago. I found out about it just now."

Theo faced me, still holding my hand with one of theirs and placing the other on my knee. "What did she do?"

"When I was a baby, my parts weren't exactly a vagina or a penis.

The doctors had my mom pick one and they did surgery on me. She consented to it. She let them cut me up without a real medical reason, just to get me to be 'normal'. It's got me so fucked up."

"So they did surgery on you when you were a baby to give you a typical vagina?"

I nodded, staring blankly into space.

They looked at me, then leaned back against the wall. "That's fucked."

"Yeah."

"Would you have wanted them to do it, if you had a choice?"

"I don't know. I'm just mad that I never got the choice. I know I'm a girl, but that was part of me, how I was. And it wasn't good enough for my mom, so she changed it. Just like everything else about me she didn't like, she tried to change me. I was never good enough."

They brushed my now soaking hair out of my face and kissed my forehead. "Fuck her, she's the one that's not good enough. She should've accepted you the way that you were."

I stared down at my hands, wondering how much of me she would've cut away if she didn't like it. Thinking about all the pieces of myself I'd let go of to make her happy, to fit in the box she'd created for me.

"Would you still be with me, if they'd left me alone? If my parts didn't perfectly fit 'girl'?"

"What kind of question is that, Alex? Of course I would, I love you, not just your vagina. You're my perfect person. I wouldn't love you any differently if your parts were different."

I sighed. They held me on such a pedestal, sometimes it was hard not to fall off. "I won't ever let that happen again, the sex like that. I hurt you, I'm sorry."

They kissed my shoulder and then rested their head on it. I put
an arm around their shoulder and rested my head on theirs, letting
the water wash away how dirty, how wrong I felt. Here, with them,
I was perfect.

CHAPTER THIRTEEN

It was Saturday morning, and we were headed to the dog shelter. Theo was getting their dog, and I was so excited to pick it out with them. After everything that had happened, we both needed this distraction, this joy. Something positive to combat the sea of negativity that had been pelting us the past couple months. Monica pulled into the parking lot of the shelter and Theo eagerly jumped out of the car, me shortly behind them. They had this amazingly child-like grin on their face, like nothing could stop the joy they were about to experience.

They rushed up to the front desk just in time for Monica to step out of the car in the parking lot. I laughed, their usual bashful shyness when it came to service desks had disintegrated.

"Can we look at the dogs, please?" they asked, breathless.

The guy at the desk smiled and nodded, walking up to a door and unlocking it, signaling us to follow just as Monica got in the door. Theo was right behind him as he led us to a back room full of kennels.

"Have a look around, come get me if you need any help," the guy said, then walked back to his post at the desk.

Barks and whines erupted all around us, many dogs eagerly pawing at the chain-link of their cages, vying for our attention. I was instantly drawn to this little Pomeranian with the fluffiest tail that was spinning in circles at the door of its cage. I knelt down and put my hand up to the door, the dog eagerly licking at my fingers.

"Aw, T, look at this one!"

Theo was at my side in an instant. "Aw, it's cute." They knelt down next to me and pressed their hand to the cage just as I had, the Pomeranian moving to lick their hand as well.

After a minute, Theo got up to look around some more, but I stayed with the pom, completely captivated by its teddy-bear-esque looks. Eventually, I was able to tear myself away and browsed through the other cages. An old-looking collie, a few adorable boxers with huge underbites, looking to be out of the same litter. A rascally looking chihuahua, a few mixed breeds that all looked sweet as pie. I had no idea how Theo would decide, but I was secretly hoping they'd circle back to the Pomeranian.

Until I walked up to the cage where Theo was standing, staring down at the dog inside. It was a chocolate lab, wagging its tail with its head hanging low, the biggest eyes I'd ever seen on a dog. It had shining, thick fur that was broken up by the scars on its left hip that led to a stump. It was missing its left back leg, and Theo was in love. All hopes of the Pomeranian were dashed. They knelt down and the dog hesitantly came closer, its huge, sad eyes winning over my heart just as they had Theo's.

"Do you want me to get the guy to take it out?" I asked softly, putting one hand on Theo's shoulder.

They nodded, eyes still locked on the dog.

I poked my head out the door and waved at the guy. "Hey, can we take one of them out?"

"Of course." He hopped up from the desk and grabbed a worn rope leash that was hanging on the wall. His smile faded when we stopped in front of the lab's cage, and he tensed up a little.

"Um…"

"What's wrong?" Theo looked up at him.

"She just uh, she's not a fan of guys. We usually have one of the girls that works here take care of her, but I'm the only one here today."

Slowly, he stepped up to the kennel, and the dog's eyes went from sad to fierce. Her tail stopped wagging, and a snarl came over her face as she growled at him.

Monica looked apprehensive, "Theo, maybe it's best if we look at another—"

"Can I try?" Theo stood up and held their hand out for the leash.

The guy handed them the leash, then slowly opened the door to the kennel, careful to keep the mesh between him and the dog. Theo knelt down again, and the dog wagged her tail while eyeing the guy now standing behind the mesh door.

"Hey, it's okay. I don't like guys either," Theo cooed, creeping closer to the dog until they were able to hook the leash onto her collar.

They held out a hand that she timidly sniffed, then they did something that took my breath away. They rolled up one of their pant legs, revealing the scars that they almost always kept hidden from the world.

"See? I'm like you."

The dog sniffed and then licked at Theo's scars, as if trying to heal them. Theo then petted the dog on the head, running their hand gently down her back, and she leaned into them, stepping forward to lick Theo's face.

Theo looked up at Monica, "Please, Mom? I want this one."

"What about Seth, and then when you have Jeremy over? I just don't want anyone getting hurt." She glanced up at the guy from the front desk. "Has she ever bitten anyone?"

"She's snapped at a few of us guys that work here, but never gotten a direct bite. We would've had to put her down if she did."

Theo's eyes widened and they pleaded, "I'll train her Mom, I promise. I'll tell her Seth and Jeremy are cool."

"I don't think that's exactly how it works."

"She'll listen to me! Watch." Theo stood up, holding the leash in their hand, then turned to the dog, "Can you sit, girl? Sit."

Almost immediately, the dog folded her hind leg and sat down, looking up at Theo, waiting for their approval.

"Good girl!" They knelt down and wrapped their arms around the dog, patting her head.

I swear the dog smiled, whining a bit while licking at Theo's face.

"You're really stuck on this one, huh?" Monica was giving in.

Theo took that as a yes, and a grin even bigger than the one they'd come in with crept across their face.

Monica resigned. "All right." She looked back at the desk guy, "We'll take this one."

"Okay, let me just scoot around here." He sidestepped way around the dog, her teeth baring only for a second before Theo placed a hand gently on her head.

We followed the guy back out to the lobby, where he positioned himself safely behind the desk and started pulling out some paperwork for Monica to sign.

Theo wasn't concerned with the paperwork, no, they were on the ground in front of the desk cooing at and petting the dog as she eagerly licked at their face. I held out a hand for the dog to sniff and after doing so, she nuzzled me and placed her head under my hand.

Front desk guy smiled. "Huh. I've never seen her this happy."

The dog wagged her tail as Theo led her back to the car. I got in the front seat so that they could sit with the dog in the back.

"Can we go to the pet store to get her stuff?"

"Maybe it's best if we bring her home first, until we get her a little more trained. I think public interactions might be a little too much."

"I wanna let her pick out her toys, though. I don't know what she likes."

Monica sighed. "Theo, I know you see the best in this dog and you're excited, but what I saw was an aggressive reaction to the presence of a guy. What if there's a guy in the store? In an environment that's already overwhelming? It's too much."

"Okay," Theo said, resigned. "Can she stay in the car with you while I get her some things?"

"I think that's a better idea." Monica gave Theo a weak smile as we drove to the nearest pet store.

I got out with Theo as Monica handed them her credit card. A dangerous move. We approached the store and Theo grabbed a cart. "Okay, what do dogs need? Food, bed, toys, harness, treats…"

I laughed a little. They never got this excited over shopping for human things. We went inside and Theo picked out the biggest, softest looking bed first. It was almost as big as they were, and they struggled to get it into the cart. I grabbed the other side and helped stuff it in. Next, we went down the food aisle, Theo picking out a big bag of food as well as a few different types of treats and some bones and a bully stick. The cart was already overflowing, and we hadn't even gotten through half the list Theo had laid out when we walked in.

"Monica's gonna kill us."

Theo waved a hand. "I never ask her for money, it's okay."

We walked down the aisle that was filled with leashes, harnesses, and collars. Theo looked through the selection, "I think blue would be pretty on her." They picked out a light teal set of three.

Then we made our way through the toy aisle and Theo looked overwhelmed, taking in all the different options. "How will I know what she likes?"

I shrugged my shoulders, "All dogs like balls, right? Maybe we start there."

They nodded, picking out a few tennis balls. Then, they picked up a stuffed squirrel. "This is cute," they said and tossed it in the cart. They picked out a few more random toys.

We started walking towards the check out when a row of bandanas caught Theo's eye and they stopped, grabbing a light blue one with ducks on it. They smiled as they showed it to me, eager to dress up their new friend.

Once we were up at the register, the cashier took one look at the cart and asked with a chuckle, "New dog?"

Theo nodded, breaking eye contact with the cashier to look at our haul. "Damn, Al, you're right. Mom's gonna be mad."

"There's a discount if you got it from a shelter," the cashier interjected.

"Yes, please. We just came from the shelter. She's a pretty chocolate lab."

The cashier nodded, "Labs are good dogs."

Theo smiled, but it slowly faded as the cashier rang up the items, the total coming to over $200, the discount knocking off about $30.

"Yikes." They handed the cashier the card and they settled the total, Theo taking back the card and pushing the cart out the door.

When we got back to the car, Theo asked Monica to pop the

trunk and they crammed everything inside, for a second I thought they'd have to jump on it to get it to fit. I brought the cart back as they finished getting everything inside, then hopped in the front seat while Theo took their place in the back with the dog.

I leaned into the back a little to see Theo with the bandana, collar, and leash they'd picked out. They took off the generic and ragged looking ones from the shelter and put the shiny new things on the dog.

"Look how beautiful you are." Theo grinned.

"What're you gonna name her?" I asked.

Theo squinted at the dog, then their grin returned. "Dulce."

I recognized the Spanish, but didn't know the translation. "What's that mean?"

"Sweet, like chocolate."

I smiled. "I like it."

We were home before too long, and Theo hopped out of the car, Dulce at their side. Monica popped the trunk and came around the back, seeing Theo's unhinged shopping spree haul for the first time.

"I don't want to know how much this cost me, do I?" She raised an eyebrow at Theo and they shrank a little.

"Probably not."

She sighed, "Well, I'll see it later on the credit card bill. I'll try not to get too mad." She patted Theo on the shoulder and pulled the dog bed from the trunk to take inside.

Theo picked up the huge bag of dog food, and I struggled to get all the bags on one arm so I could carry them all inside after shutting the trunk. I got inside and dragged the bags up the stairs, following Theo into their room where Monica had already set the bed in the corner. We shut the door and Theo let Dulce off the leash, and she instantly had her nose in the bags.

Theo rummaged through the bags with her, pulling out the bully stick and taking the sticker off.

"Can you sit, Dulce?"

Dulce looked up at them, not registering the command at first. She caught sight of the treat in Theo's hand and then sat down.

"Good girl!" Theo handed her the stick and she took it eagerly, walking over to the bed and lying down with it.

I helped Theo unpack the rest of the stuff, and they pulled a plastic bin out of their closet to use for all of the toys. They brought the treats downstairs where they'd left the dog food, and found a place for everything in the pantry. They couldn't resist giving Dulce a bone to go with her bully stick, and she was completely engrossed in her treats as Theo sat down next to her and ran their hands across her soft fur.

"What do you think happened to her?" I asked, realizing we'd never asked at the shelter.

"I dunno, it doesn't really matter to me. Whatever it is, it's her past. It's not who she is. She's my dog now, whatever happened won't happen again."

There was a knock on the door, and Dulce stopped chewing on her bone and stared up at it, eyes narrowing. The door opened and we saw it was Seth, Dulce was immediately on guard. She bared her teeth and Seth froze in place.

"Damn, did you get a killer? I just wanted to come see."

"The guy at the shelter said she doesn't like guys. Come in, I'll try telling her you're cool."

He snickered as he slid inside the door. "Your dog's a bouncer. I get it."

Theo rolled their eyes, but when Seth took a step inside, Dulce rose to her feet and started barking. A big, powerful sound that echoed in my ears. She growled between barks, and Theo put their arms around her.

"Hey, it's okay. Seth's cool. He's a good guy. There aren't a lot, but he's one of them."

Dulce continued barking, and Theo picked up her bone and handed it to Seth. "Maybe if you have a treat she'll calm down."

He sat down in Theo's desk chair, not daring to get any closer. Theo pet Dulce on the head, trying to calm her down.

"Hey, look, he's got a treat."

Her barks slowly died down as she realized Seth wasn't making any moves towards her. She didn't dare get closer to Seth, but sat back down, whining and licking Theo's face. After she sat for a few minutes, Theo got up and stood next to Seth, putting a hand on his shoulder.

"Come here, Dulce, he's got a treat for you."

Seth held out the bone with his hand, and Dulce backed up, the hair around her neck ruffling as her muzzle turned into a snarl.

Theo ruffled Seth's hair and threw their arm around his shoulder, "Really, he's cool, I promise."

Dulce sat down again, unmoving from her bed across the room from where Seth was sitting. She eyed him warily, and refused to go closer and retrieve the bone.

"Wait, shit, is she missing a leg?"

Theo sighed, giving up on getting Dulce to get closer to Seth. They took the bone from his hands and sat back down next to her, and she warily sniffed the bone before taking it.

"Yeah. Who would I be if I didn't pick a dog as fucked up as me?"

"Some guy must've fucked her up pretty bad, if me just being here scares her."

Theo pet Dulce on the head and smiled at Seth. "She just needs some convincing, and some time. She'll get used to you."

"For now, I'm just gonna err on the side of not making any sudden movements." He slowly got up from the chair, and Dulce followed him with her eyes as he left the room.

She visibly relaxed once he left.

"Do you think she's got it in her to bite someone?" I asked, nervous at the prospect of the dog getting taken away when Theo was already so attached to her.

"I dunno, we just gotta take things slow. She needs some training. But she trusts me, so we've got a good start."

They got up from the floor, leaving Dulce to settle in. Sitting down next to me, they put their hands on my shoulders and pulled me in for a kiss. I wrapped my arms around their waist and pulled them in close to me, kissing them back.

"What was that for?" I asked.

"I'm sorry, I know you liked the Pomeranian."

I ran my hands through their hair, "Don't be sorry, I just want you to be happy. And this dog makes you really happy."

CHAPTER FOURTEEN

Harriet had been texting me to meet up, and I wanted to give Theo some time alone to work on training Dulce. So I walked into Best Boba at eleven AM on Sunday to see Harriet sitting at a table near the window rather than the long table in the middle of the shop where we usually sat as a whole group. I ordered a tea – strawberry milk tea with strawberry bubbles – and sat down across from her.

"No Theo?" she asked.

I shook my head, "They just got a new dog, I figured hanging out with you would give them some bonding time."

"Oh! That's cool, what kind of dog?"

"Chocolate lab."

"Cute."

I nodded, taking a sip of my tea.

"How're you doing? The last time I saw you in person I was holding your hair back while you puked in a school toilet."

My face flushed. "Yeah, sorry about that."

"Nothing to be sorry for. I just wanna know that you're okay."

"Things have been… well, kinda shitty. I had a talk with my mom."

"How'd it go?"

"Not great. I found something out that's got me kinda fucked up."

"What is it? If you don't mind me asking."

I paused. Did I really want to tell her this? How would she react, finding out I was intersex? I didn't want it going around school, not that I thought Harriet was a gossip, but adding someone to the small circle of people that knew felt dangerous somehow.

"If I tell you, you won't tell anyone else? Not even the group."

She leaned back in her chair, keeping eye contact with me. "I can keep a secret. I'll take it to my grave."

I gave a little laugh and rolled my eyes – more dramatic than I'd expected, but she was sincere.

"I'm intersex. I have androgen insensitivity syndrome." I left out the part about the surgery, I wasn't ready to tell people that.

"I… wow, yeah, that's kinda big." She leaned in a little, placing her hands around her cup of tea. "If you've always felt like a girl, though, that doesn't change anything, right?"

I shrugged, looking down at my tea.

"Have you? Always felt like a girl?"

"I mean, yeah. I know I'm still a girl, it's just so much to wrap my head around. What would it have been like if my mom had chosen for me to be a boy? Would I be trans?"

"Hold up, what do you mean chosen?"

Shit. I hadn't meant to bring up the implications that came with that. Now I had to tell her.

"They had my mom pick. They did surgery on me as a baby. That's what I really found out when I talked to her."

"That's so fucked up, that should've been your choice, not theirs."

I nodded. "She literally had pieces of me cut away to make me what she wanted. I always felt like I wasn't what she'd hoped for, and that really solidified it. Right when I was born I wasn't good enough."

"Do you think maybe the doctors pressured her into it? I've heard that the medical community sometimes makes it sound like a necessity, not a choice. It's partly on her for not doing more research, but if she really believed what the doctors told her at face value, maybe it wasn't so much getting rid of parts of you she didn't like. Maybe she thought she was taking care of you."

I gave Harriet a hard glare. I didn't know why she was trying to defend my mother right now. Everything about the situation was so screwed up – her take was plausible, but I needed to be mad at someone, and my mother felt like the right choice.

Harriet raised her hands. "I don't mean it's not still fucked up, what they did. I'm just saying maybe there wasn't malice on your mother's part. But I don't know her, I could be wrong."

"She beat me with a belt when she found out I was dating Theo. That feels pretty malicious."

"I'm sorry," Harriet recanted.

"My whole life, I tried to be what she wanted. I'm sick of it, trying to fit in the box she put me in. I just want to be me. Why can't she love *me?*" Tears threatened to spill out of my eyes, so I stopped and took a deep breath to try and tamp them down.

Harriet placed a hand over one of mine. "I'm sorry, my parents are pretty chill, I don't know what that rejection's like. I bet it fucking sucks though."

"What did your parents do when they found out you were queer? What do good parents do?"

"My mom just asked if I still wanted kids, my dad hugged me. When I told them, I was afraid they'd be upset, but it never crossed my mind that they'd act on it. They always told me they'd love me no matter what, so I guess I held onto that."

"I'd like to think, if my dad were here, he would've stopped my mom."

"Did your dad die?"

"No, he left when I was thirteen. Took the coward's way out, left me to deal with my mom's resentment. He always loved me, but apparently not enough to stay." A tear fought its way out of the corner of my eye, and I wiped it away quickly, hoping Harriet wouldn't notice.

"You don't have contact with him? He just split?"

I shook my head. "My parents went to court, I assume for custody, and my mom managed to get sole custody of us. I don't know that my dad fought too hard. I never got letters or anything from him, but I think even if he sent them my mom would've thrown them out. So I don't know if he tried at all."

"Do you ever think about trying to find him, now that you're out of there? She can't stop you now that you're living with Theo."

"Huh, no, everything's been so hectic, it hasn't crossed my mind. How would I find him?"

"You can find anyone on the internet. C'mon, let me see your phone. What's his name?"

I handed her my phone, "Johnathan Kensington."

She tapped away on my phone, scrolled for a bit, and then turned the phone screen to face me. "This him? He looks like you."

There was a picture of my dad with a Jack Russell terrier, looking happy as anything. Why was he so happy without me? I took the phone and shook my head, mom never would've let him get a dog. "It was that easy this whole time?"

"The power of the internet."

I tapped on the profile, but before scrolling down I thought better of doing it now, in front of Harriet. I had no idea what I'd find, I wasn't sure if I was ready. "Thank you." I breathed, then slid the phone back into my pocket.

Harriet nodded, "Let me know how it goes. I'm rooting for you."

I sighed, taking a sip of my tea. "How's school been for you? We still fight our way through the halls every day, poor Elliot's nose still isn't healed, and they keep trying to break it again."

She shook her head. "I fly under the radar pretty well. No one's caught on yet."

"I wish we could be like that. Theo was already a target before they started transitioning, and I wasn't going to make them keep us a secret at school on top of hiding it from my mom, so I got dragged in pretty quick."

"What made them a target before? They seem pretty able to hold their own, I don't know why people choose to mess with them at all, let alone before they transitioned."

"They kinda brought it on themself, they were almost like a vigilante. They didn't pick fights, but they'd step in real fast if they saw someone else getting picked on. The bullies always wanted to get back at them, so they became a target, even though they had the strength to fend them off, it didn't stop a group of shitheads from trying."

"Noble."

I scoffed. "I always hated it, the fighting. They were too reckless. Now they've got no choice. They're much better than they used to be, but there's still times when I can see them ready to snap, and then it'll get ugly. I basically play interference. The bullies don't get how lucky they are that I'm there."

"Why not just let Theo loose? Those guys deserve it."

"You make them sound like a wild animal."

"Sorry. That's not how I meant it. I mean, why stop Theo from putting an end to it?"

"Because it would be an end for them too. They'd get expelled at best, arrested at worst. When they lose control, there's no stopping them without force. And they're strong, really strong."

"They'd lose it that bad?"

"Yes. I've seen it. They're a lot better than they used to be, they try so hard to keep their anger under control now. But there's an ugly side of them if they're pushed too far."

"Would they ever hurt someone they cared about?" Harriet's face had slowly contorted to concern over the course of the conversation.

"No, never. It's when people they care about are threatened that they really have a hard time keeping their anger under control. They love fiercely."

Harriet leaned back in her chair, relief taking over her expression. "They kinda gave me that vibe."

I nodded, taking another sip of my tea.

Harriet exhaled, looking around the shop for a second and then turning back to me, "So, hey, since school sucks, our group kinda does this thing instead of prom."

"Like what?"

"Well, this year, we're going to have a party at my house, fun decorations and all. You, Theo, and Jeremy should come."

"Thanks, yeah, I'll talk to them about it."

"It's usually way more fun than any school dance I've ever been to, but I gave up going after middle school so I guess I wouldn't know now."

"I've only ever been at dances with random guys that were just performing to get sex out of me. I'd like to go with Theo, but I don't know how safe it would be. Most teachers are pretty condescending about them, I know queer couples are usually frowned upon."

"I heard last year they kicked a lesbian couple out for dancing together, pretty fucked up."

"Ugh." I wrinkled my nose, annoyed at how backwards this school was.

"Yeah, at my place we can just be ourselves, with all our friends, and not worry about any of that. We can still get all dressed up and have fun. Plus, we get better snacks." She laughed, leaning back in her chair.

I smiled. "Thanks for inviting us, I might drag Theo out even if they're reluctant, it sounds fun. Jeremy's usually happy to go anywhere he's welcome."

Harriet nodded, smiling as she finished off her tea.

————

When I got home, Theo wasn't there. They'd sent me a text letting me know they were out for a run with Dulce. I was glad the bonding was seemingly going well. I made my way up the stairs, stripping off my jeans and changing into one of Theo's oversized hoodies and a pair of shorts before diving into bed and curling up beneath the blankets.

It was like I didn't have energy for anything these days, just the basics were so exhausting. I was happy to be curled up and relaxing. Pulling out my phone, I was reminded of my dad's profile that Harriet had found so quickly. I couldn't believe I hadn't thought to look for him this whole time. I guess I assumed that if he didn't reach out for me, I couldn't reach back. My mom discouraged any talk about him, so I'd shoved it out of my mind all this time.

Taking in a deep breath, I opened the profile again and began scrolling. He still lived in the city according to his info. The idea of seeing him again filled me with joy. At least, until I started scrolling further. It wasn't just a dog he'd brought into his life. There were pictures of him with another woman.

And a baby.

He'd gone and started a whole new family without me.

My heart sank, and I could physically feel the jealousy that rose within me, turning my stomach. I felt a little silly, being jealous of a baby, but this baby had all my father's attention, and I had none. I hadn't spoken to him in three years, and he'd gone and moved on.

Was I not good enough for him either? Had all the affection I'd gotten from him as a kid been fake, manufactured?

He looked so happy without me.

I jumped as the door opened, Theo bursting inside with Dulce right behind them. They unhooked her leash and she flopped down on her bed in the corner of the room as Theo walked over to me and kissed my forehead.

They were drenched in sweat but had the biggest smile on their face, one that I couldn't be mad at.

"She's so good on a leash! Didn't pay attention to anything but me the whole time we were running, and she kept up so well! It's like she's not even missing a leg." They were so excited, I didn't have the heart to tell them about my dad and tried to mask the face of contempt that had come over me while I'd been scrolling.

Theo got up and stripped off their sweaty tank top, revealing their binder underneath.

"T, you ran in that?"

They looked back at me and then glanced downwards, their voice getting small as if they were anticipating the reprimand. "Yeah."

"Babe, c'mon, you know it's bad for you. You're gonna fuck up your breathing."

"I know, but I just get so damn dysphoric without it. Those tight sports bras we got don't really help. I wish I could just get this shit cut off."

"Hasn't Monica been helping you with that?"

"Yeah, but there's so many goddamn hoops you have to jump through to get top surgery. She's trying, but it's still taking forever. They don't even recognize agender as a thing, so I have to tell all the therapists I'm a guy to get them to approve it. I hate all the 'he/him' I get, it's not as bad as 'she/her', but it still doesn't feel right. I just know I'll feel so much better once it's over."

"God, I'm sorry the system is such shit. You need it, that should be enough for them. It's your body, why do so many people have to have such a say in it? Why is it so hard for you to get a surgery you actually need when they'll just go and cut up babies willy nilly?" Woah, that anger had come out of nowhere, my voice had gotten harsh.

Theo sat down on the edge of the bed and ran their hand through my hair, kissing me on the forehead again. "The system's fucked."

I gave them a weak smile and touched their arm lightly, but recoiled when it came away wet. "Gross, get in the shower you loser."

They rolled their eyes at me, then got up from the bed and pulled a change of clothes from their dresser. They left for the bathroom and Dulce let out a little whine as they closed the door behind them.

"It's okay, we're cool, right?" I said, and Dulce got up from the bed, walking over to me and nuzzling my hand for a pet. "Yeah, we're cool."

I turned back to my phone as Dulce went back to her bed. Opening a message to my dad, I sucked in a deep breath, anxiety rising within me as I stared at the blank text box. What did I say to a dad that hadn't contacted me in three years? Did I just start a conversation, like nothing had happened? Would it be weird to ask him to meet me somewhere? Would he even want me, now that he had his new family?

I must've been staring at it for a lot longer than I thought, because the shower shut off and Theo came back into the room before I'd even typed a single word. I was so focused that I barely noticed as they sat down next to me in their fresh pair of joggers and clean tank top, smelling of vanilla. They had just finished applying lotion to their hands and face when they looked over at me.

"Hey, you okay?"

"Hm?" I didn't look up.

They leaned in, waving a hand in front of my phone. "What're you so invested in? You've got that face you get when you're thinking too hard."

I dropped the phone on the bed, message screen still open, and rubbed my face with my hands while groaning. "Harriet found my dad for me."

They leaned back, picking up the phone and squinting at the screen, bringing it close to their face as they adjusted their glasses. "Shit, I didn't know you were looking for him. Are you gonna message him?"

"I wasn't really, I mentioned something about him when I was talking to Harriet earlier and she found him after looking for like, two seconds. I can't believe I didn't do it myself before."

"I guess it's easier now that your mom can't interfere."

"Yeah. I don't know what to say to him. It looks like he has a whole new family now. What if he doesn't want to see me?"

"Al, he was crazy about you, of course he'd want to see you."

"Then why didn't he contact me at all in these three years?"

"Maybe he did? Maybe your mom hid it, or wouldn't let him, or something."

"Yeah, I keep thinking that, but I still don't know what to say. He looks so happy with his new family. What if I ruin it?"

"You won't ruin anything. Do you want help? How about 'Hey dad, can I see you?' Something simple. You don't have any explaining to do."

"Every time I go to type letters my hands get all shaky and my chest gets tight, I don't know why it's like this. I guess I'm afraid he doesn't love me anymore."

"I doubt that. Just from how he was around you that I saw, I don't think anything could take away that love."

I sighed, "Can you type it? I just can't."

Theo nodded and tapped away at my phone, then turned it to me. "All you gotta do is hit send."

I took the phone from their hands, my heart fluttering in my chest, causing me to get light-headed as I stared at the message. The anxiety built within me until I took a deep breath, held it, and then tapped 'send', promptly dropping the phone onto the bed.

"Why was that so hard?" I put my hands over my face again, grumbling. My emotions felt like they were dialed up to ten lately.

Theo got into bed, pulling the blanket over themself and wrapping me up in their arms. They kissed me on the neck, sending shivers down my spine. I turned to face them and kissed them on the lips when I heard a soft buzz as my phone went off.

I sat up instantly, digging through the covers for my discarded phone. My mind was racing as I tapped the screen awake and eagerly checked my messages.

It was Harriet, sending me the details of the party in a couple weeks. I sighed and flopped back down in the bed, and Theo brushed the hair out of my face.

"Not him?"

"Not him."

They leaned up on one elbow, looking over me as they stroked my hair. "He'll text. Try not to worry about it."

"Easier said than done."

"I know."

There was a silence as they continued stroking my hair. I looked up at them – they made everything so tender. Before I was with them, I didn't like touching that didn't lead anywhere. Now, I'd grown to love it, because I knew how much it meant to them. Loving touch was something they had been so deprived of. it seemed this really was the first time they'd had it, and they relished it. And, because I loved them, I grew to adore and savor their soft touch, even when it didn't lead to sex. Sometimes, the touching, skin to skin, was the best part.

But god, did it make me want more. That part was hard sometimes.

"T, can I ask you something?"

"Of course."

"Do you even like sex?"

They stopped stroking my hair, but rested their arm across my waist, not recoiling at my inquiry. "I like it with you. I've never wanted it with anyone else. I know I don't want it as often as you do, I'm sorry."

I shook my head, "No, that's not something to be sorry about. I was just wondering, because sometimes it feels like you'd just rather hold me."

"Sometimes I would. I like sex because I can make you feel

good though."

"Is that the only thing you like about it? You don't like the way it makes you feel?"

"I don't think I feel it the same way you do. The part before, when we're kissing and holding each other, I love that part. It's my favorite. I get to feel close to you, like nothing can separate us. The rest is mostly about making you feel good. I want you to feel that same closeness I get out of holding you."

"You don't like it when I touch you there?"

"I like it sometimes, not all the time though."

"I want you to tell me, when you don't like it. Don't do things just because you think I'll like it."

"You liking it is what makes it good for me."

"T, do you think you might be asexual?"

"I think I'm demisexual. I've never felt that kind of attraction to anyone but you. I do feel it with you, sometimes I really do want it for myself too. I just don't think I want it in the same way you do."

I laid there, staring at the ceiling for a minute, then threw my arms around the back of Theo's neck and pulled them in for a kiss.

"Is it okay, that I am? I want to be enough for you."

I held them close to my face, my eyes half closed as I looked up at them. "You'll always be enough."

They sighed, letting their body relax against mine as they lay on top of me. They were really heavy for someone as small as they were, but the pressure felt good.

My phone buzzed again.

Theo got off me as I scrambled to find it, lost in the sea of sheets and blankets. I heard it fall to the ground as I lifted up a small throw, then dangled myself off the side of the bed to get it. I almost fell, but Theo grabbed me at the last second and pulled me back up onto the bed. They giggled at me and I smiled back, until I glanced at my phone screen.

"It's him."

"Open it!"

"I'm scared."

My hands shook as I unlocked my phone and the icon of my dad's profile came up. I hovered over the button to open the message, willing myself to tap the screen, but unable to actually do it.

Before I could stop them, Theo leaned over and pushed down my thumb, causing me to tap the icon. I sent them a harsh glare as my stomach churned. I wasn't ready for this. What if he said no, what if he—

"Hi, honey, I'd love to come see you. When can we meet up? I'm free every day after six."

I was *so* ready for this.

Grinning, I turned the phone so that Theo could see. They smiled. "See? I told you it would be okay."

I sent back a message, and we made plans to see each other that Thursday around seven PM. Four days. In four days I was going to see my dad for the first time in three years.

CHAPTER FIFTEEN

What I wasn't ready for was school the next morning. I felt a rush of anxiety as we walked inside and saw Kyle and his group loitering in front of the lockers. Theo looked back at Elliot and I, making hand signals like we were some special ops crew. We were going to split up today, Elliot ducking through adjoining classrooms, me looping around the nurse's office, and Theo walking right by them, hoping they wouldn't notice.

I hid around the corner, watching as Theo walked by them. Kyle was preoccupied, babbling on about some girl he'd actually gotten to sleep with him. Kyle got laid, so we got a pass. We met up in the next hallway over and Elliot unironically jumped for joy.

"I can't believe that worked! Do you think it'll work every day?"

"Doubt it," Theo said flatly as they opened their locker.

We got startled as Theo closed their locker, revealing Jeremy, who'd been standing behind it. He had tears in his eyes, but that wasn't the first thing we noticed. It was the handprint-sized bruise on his cheek that caught us off guard. Theo immediately took Jeremy's face in their hands, examining the damage.

"Who did this?"

"You know," he muttered, shrugging them off and wiping at the tears that threatened to spill over. "Can I stay at your place tonight?"

"Of course. I don't want you going back there tonight."

"It was my fault." His voice was small, barely audible in the chatter of the halls.

"No, Jer, it wasn't. There's no reason for her to put her hands on you."

He leaned in, avoiding eye contact. "I told her I like guys."

"What? I mean, she still shouldn't have hit you, but why would you tell her?"

"She was being nice for once. She wasn't drunk. She was asking if I was interested in any girls at school and then it just kinda slipped. I didn't mean to tell her, I was just so happy she was talking to me like an actual person and I… I trusted too much. It hurts so much more knowing she hit me sober, she knew exactly what she was doing."

Theo placed a hand on Jeremy's shoulder. "I'm sorry. You can stay more than just tonight if you need to."

He nodded, staring at the floor. The bell rang, and we all went our separate ways to our classes. I sat alone in my history class, just thinking about what Jeremy had said. Why did parents have to be so cruel? Why did it matter so much who we fell in love with?

My heart skipped a beat as I thought about my dad. What will he think about me dating Theo? Will he walk away, shunning me for my sexuality? I didn't think he had it in him to hurt me the way my mom had, but people were so unpredictable when confronted with news they didn't want to hear. Especially from their children. My love was seen as an act of rebellion by my mother, not as the truth that it was. I fell short of her expectations. Did my father even have any expectations left of me? Or had he let go of them when he found his new family? Did he care what I did anymore?

The bell rang again, and I realized I hadn't heard anything that was taught the entire class. I shook my head, trying to focus on what was happening in the moment and not all the fears and emotions that were swirling around in my mind. I'd have to deal with those on Thursday. For now, I just needed to get through the school day.

I managed to make it through to lunch, grabbing a limp salad that I wasn't hungry for and sitting down at our usual table. Theo, Jeremy, and Elliot joined me, and for once it seemed that Theo was the least in their head out of all of us. I picked at my salad with the flimsy plastic fork I'd been given, not having the will to bring any of it to my mouth. Jeremy was staring down at his food, a distant gaze in his eyes that said he wasn't really looking at anything in front of him. His shoulders were hunched over in a posture that begged for people to leave him alone. Elliot was looking between us, as if unsure of what to say, until Theo tapped him on the shoulder with their phone.

"Look at my dog! Isn't she beautiful?"

Elliot eagerly took the phone and his face lit up. "She's adorable. What's her name?"

"Dulce. I just got her Saturday. She's the best."

Nodding, Elliot handed Theo back the phone. "I'll have to come meet her some time."

"Jer, you wanna see?"

Jeremy didn't answer, eyes still glazed over and fixed in front of him.

"Jeremy, hey? What's up?"

I took my attention off my limp salad and gently rested a hand on Jeremy's shoulder. He jumped, as if I'd hit him. He looked over at me, then around the table, blinking back tears for the second time today.

"Sorry. I'm just… thinking."

"About your mom?" Theo asked.

He nodded, rubbing at his eyes with his hands.

"Seriously, she can fuck off, Jeremy. She doesn't deserve you, the way she treats you. You shouldn't feel bad for things she does."

"I know, but she's still my mom. I want her to love me."

His words rang true to my core. I wanted so badly to hate my mother for what she'd done to me, but at the same time I craved her love, and not having it had really messed with me these past couple months. I'd never wanted something so badly that it hurt to not have it before, other than when my father left. I knew exactly how Jeremy felt. I'd been rejected over the same thing, really.

I rested a hand on his shoulder. "Jer, I get it. It hurts."

He nodded, staring down at his food again.

"Hey! Missed you fuckers this morning!"

Kyle. He never came around during lunch. Theo glared at him as he approached our table with a couple of his friends flocking in behind him.

"You guys think you can get away without saying hi?" He cracked his knuckles as he stepped up to the table.

"Why are you so obsessed with us?" I snorted at him.

Kyle snickered, and then flipped Jeremy's tray into his lap, effectively covering him in mac and cheese. He worked his way around the table, grabbing Elliot's still-bruised nose. Elliot yelped, and Theo had enough. They stood from the table and ripped Kyle's hands away from Elliot, standing merely an inch from Kyle's face.

"Fuck off, Kyle."

Kyle shoved them, and I saw the flash of anger in their eyes. I got up to diffuse the situation, just like I always did, and stepped between Theo and Kyle.

"What, your girlfriend's gotta fight your battles for you? You fucking pussy."

"God, why do I bother protecting you, Kyle?" I didn't really do it for him, I did it so that Theo wouldn't end up expelled for what they inevitably did to him if they were pushed too far. But you'd think he'd be smart enough to know I wasn't fighting for Theo, they could take care of that all on their own. He'd walked away with enough bruises to know that.

Kyle stared past me and at Theo. Then, without breaking eye contact, drew up the spit in his mouth and then spit in Theo's food.

"You're disgusting." I wrinkled my nose at him, not daring to move and unleash Theo's wrath.

"What're you gonna do about it, pussy?"

This time, Kyle shoved me, and Theo caught me as I fell back into them.

Something broke inside me. Why did he come after us, relentlessly, every day, when most of the time he didn't win? Why was he so adamant on making our lives hell? Why did he get to judge us for who we were, when he was one of the scummiest people I'd ever met? Why did he think he could get away with hurting us? Why *did* he get away with hurting us?

We were undesirables, the bottom of the food chain. So he thought he could step on us, eat us alive. I'd had enough.

I rebounded, steadying my feet as Theo supported me. Then, curled my hand into a fist, thumb on the outside just like Theo had taught me. Next came the punch, and I swear my arm did it on its own. Before I knew it, Kyle was doubled over, gasping for air as I'd hit him just under the ribcage, knocking all the breath from his body.

A chorus of *"ohhhhhh"*'s rang out from various people in the cafeteria.

I'd never hit anyone before, I didn't like putting my hands on people. It didn't come naturally to me, but here, in this moment, it felt really damn good. Kyle had it coming.

"You bitch!" Kyle choked out between coughs and trying to catch his breath. His friends closed in on us, making a circle around me and Theo. Elliot was gone, and I couldn't see Jeremy. I was glad they weren't there. I didn't want them getting hurt.

Theo ducked as one of Kyle's friends tried to grab them. I felt the wind from the guy's arms brush the back of my neck, and almost turned to see what was going on when Kyle lunged at me. He grabbed me by the shoulders and instincts overcame me. I kneed him right in the crotch. Instantly, he let go of me, yowling as he went down to the ground. For a guy that played tough, he really couldn't take a hit.

Kyle's friends had gotten ahold of Theo, and they were struggling to free their arms. The anger in their eyes had shifted to panic – if there was one thing that could overwhelm them, it was feeling trapped. I ran over and started yanking at the guy's arms as Theo squirmed and flailed.

"That's enough!" A booming voice came from the door of the cafeteria.

All of our attention snapped to the teacher, with Elliot and Jeremy at her side. Theo's English teacher. At least there was one good one in this hellhole of a school. The guys holding Theo released their grip and ran in the opposite direction, towards the other entrance of the cafeteria, leaving Kyle to fend for himself. He was still whimpering on the floor.

I turned my attention to Theo, who was breathing heavily and shaking. That encounter was definitely enough to push them into a panic attack.

I gently placed a hand on their shoulder. "T, hey, it's okay. It's over."

The teacher came over to us, trying to evaluate the situation. She'd seen Theo being held back for sure, but I wasn't sure how much of the rest of it she'd been there for. At least, she seemed to understand that we weren't the offenders. Kyle managed to drag himself up from the floor, leaning on the table for support.

"Did you see what they did to me? They attacked me!"

Pathetic. Of course he'd play the victim.

"And I suppose you're going to tell me you didn't put hands on them first?" The teacher raised an eyebrow. "After what you did to Elliot the other week, I'd have a hard time believing that."

I'd never seen Kyle give up so fast. He turned and ran in the direction of his friends.

During all this, Theo had turned to the table to support themself and was now wheezing. I rubbed their back, trying to help them calm down.

"T, sit down."

They shook their head, still wheezing, closing their eyes against the tears that were trying to spill out.

"Theo, let's go to the nurse." The teacher rested a hand on their shoulder gently, guiding them away from the table and towards the hallway.

Our whole group followed, not saying anything as Theo struggled to keep air in their lungs. The walk to the nurse felt like an eternity, every step echoed through the hallway to accompany Theo's heavy breathing. Once we got there, the nurse jumped up from her desk to see how she could help. Theo made a beeline for the couch, and dropped down into the seat, covering their face with their hands.

The nurse nodded at the teacher, who made her exit now that Theo was safely inside the office. Rummaging through a locked cabinet, the nurse pulled out a bottle of Theo's medication and got a small cup of water.

Theo took it quickly, tossing back their head and swallowing the pill before the nurse even gave them the water. They took a sip but spilled most of it because of how badly they were shaking. The nurse took the cup back and rested a hand on Theo's knee.

"Let's try breathing, okay?"

Theo nodded, taking a breath in as I rubbed their back. They still held their head in their hands, but were following the nurse's count to breathe. After a few minutes, their shaking calmed along with their breath.

They leaned into me, still covering their face. "I'm so fucking tired," came muffled through their hands.

"I know, baby," I whispered.

———————

The rest of the school day was uneventful, and Theo, Jeremy, and I boarded the bus headed to Theo's house. Theo was groggy and out of it from their medication, trying hard to focus on what was happening. I held them in my arms as we waited for the bus to arrive at our destination.

As we walked in the house, Dulce came bounding down the stairs to greet us. Theo knelt on the floor and hugged her. I warily glanced at Jeremy, waiting for Dulce's negative reaction she'd shown around every other guy. Instead, when Theo let go of her, she simply walked up to Jeremy, sniffing at his feet, then nuzzling his hand for pets.

"Huh." I stood there staring, dumbfounded.

"What?" Jeremy asked.

"It's just, she's growled at every other guy I've seen her meet. It seems like she *likes* you. It's a little weird."

Jeremy knelt down as Dulce licked at his face, and Theo smiled. "Maybe she's getting better about it already."

After sufficient pets were given, Jeremy dropped his bag and sank into the couch in the living room. I dropped mine next to his and sat in the oversized loveseat, while Theo stood, staring blankly.

"T, you okay?"

They blinked quickly as their attention snapped onto me, "Yeah, I'm just really tired. I think I should take a nap."

"Come cuddle with me, you can sleep here." I scooted over and pulled a blanket from the back of the chair. They dropped their bag next to the chair and kicked off their shoes, wasting no time in cuddling up on my chest as I wrapped them in the blanket. They closed their eyes and within minutes were asleep. Dulce climbed up on the ottoman at our feet and curled up, letting out a sigh.

Jeremy clicked on the television, but turned the volume way down so as to not wake up Theo. I ran my hands through Theo's hair, watching as Jeremy switched through the channels before settling on some sci-fi movie. He took off his shoes and put his feet up on the coffee table before briefly making eye contact with me and then looking away.

"Jer, did Theo tell you what happened right before I came to stay here?"

"No," he said, eyes fixed to the television.

"My mom found out about us. She took a belt to me, tore up my back."

That pulled his attention away from the screen and he looked over at me. "Really?"

"Yeah. I'm just saying, I get it. You wanted your mom to accept you, you took a chance and trusted her. And she took your vulnerability and smashed it right back in your face. It sucks, and it's not fair. We're just living our lives, how we were meant to be. Being rejected for it by the person that's supposed to love you the most is the worst feeling in the world."

Jeremy sniffed, looking away from me again, "Why can't they just love us for who we are?"

"I don't know, I wish they would." My voice was small.

"It's so much worse that she was sober, it means she really meant to hit me. She's never done anything to me when she was sober before. I don't know if I can go home."

"Well, like Theo said, I never use the guest room, so it's open. At least this is a safe place."

"I just don't want to put Monica out. I feel bad, she just wanted one kid and somehow four fell into her lap."

"I don't think she minds. She actually loves us."

"She's too nice. She'd never say anything even if it did bother her."

"I don't think that's true, you should've seen her tell my mom off when she came here."

"Your mom came here?"

"Yeah, she started shouting at the door telling me to come home and that she'd send me some place to 'fix' me. She wants me to go to a conversion camp."

"Yikes."

"Yeah."

"And Monica went off on her?"

"Yeah, stood her ground and protected me. She said she'd never let her take me, no matter what.”

A small smile crept onto Jeremy’s face. “I hope she likes me as much as she likes you.”

“If she knew half the shit you’ve done to help and protect Theo, I think she’d like you more than me.”

He rolled his eyes and waved his hand. “You’re the one that saved their life.”

“And you’re the one that always made sure they made it home safe. It’s not a contest, Jer.”

He nodded, sinking deeper into the couch cushions. There was a silence between us as we watched television.

After a long while, Jeremy asked, “Do you still love your mom?”

I hesitated as I thought for a minute, but couldn’t help but tell the truth, “Yes.”

“Me too. It sucks.”

“It does.”

CHAPTER SIXTEEN

Today was the day. Thursday. I was going to see my dad for the first time in three years. I didn't know what to expect, didn't know how to present myself. Digging through the limited outfits I had in the closet of the guest room, I struggled to find the right thing to wear. I stared into the closet for a minute, feeling defeated, when a pair of hands wrapped around my waist and pulled me into a hug.

"What's wrong?" Theo asked.

"I don't know what to wear."

"Do you really think it'll matter to him?"

"No, I don't know… I want to look nice."

"You always look nice."

"That's what you're supposed to say."

They let me go and then started rummaging through the closet until they pulled out a casual green dress with a black belt that had a gold clasp. "What about this? I love this one, it brings out your eyes."

I took the dress from them, holding it up to myself in the mirror on the closet door. "You're sure it's not too plain?"

"You could add a necklace or something if you wanted."

I pulled open a drawer of the dresser, revealing the little bit of jewelry I'd brought with me. There were a few bracelets, some rings, and a small collection of necklaces. My eyes fell on a gold chain that matched the clasp of the belt perfectly. I picked it up and handed it to Theo, and they put it on me. Closing the door, I slipped off my jeans and t-shirt and put the dress on, adjusting it around my frame until it was comfortable.

"Can I braid your hair?"

"Please, I don't know what to do with this mess." Sitting down on the bed, I threw my hair over my shoulders. Theo picked up a brush and comb off the dresser and sat down behind me, going to work brushing the knots out of my hair. They made quick work of it, and before I knew it my hair was pulled back neatly into a loose French braid. I got up and looked in the mirror, looking myself up and down before putting on a pair of gold sandals.

"I'm ready… I guess."

I took in a deep breath as Theo wrapped their arms around me again, kissing me on the cheek. "You look beautiful."

Theo walked with me on the way to the cafe where I'd planned to meet my dad. It was a silent walk. Theo looked around at the scenery while I internally panicked about the interaction that was about to happen. Would he be the same? How much had he moved on? What would he remember about me? Had I changed too much?

I snapped back to reality when Theo stopped walking, about a block away from the cafe.

"Do you want to go from here? I don't know if you want your dad to know about us yet. I don't even know if he'd recognize me."

"Y-yeah. I'll go. But I'm going to tell him about us, I promise."

"You don't have to."

"I want to. His reaction will tell me if I really want him to be in my life again."

Suddenly, my blood ran cold.

Theo squeezed my hands in theirs. "What's wrong?"

"Do you think he knew about the surgery when I was a baby?"

"Shit, I don't know."

I felt itchy, anxiety making my skin crawl. What if he'd been in agreement with my mother's decision? What if I wasn't good enough for him either?

Theo placed their hands on my shoulders, looking up at me. "Hey, it's gonna be okay. If he turns out to be shitty, you walk away and never see him again if you want."

"I don't know if I can lose two parents like that."

They gave me a faint smile and stood on their tiptoes to kiss me on the forehead. "I'll do whatever I can to make it okay."

I drew in another deep breath before turning and walking the rest of the way to the cafe. Scanning the outdoor seating, my eyes landed on a man that felt like home. He had a short beard, which was new, but he was still the same person that had held me through sleepless nights as a child, protecting me from the monsters under my bed. He was looking down at his phone and hadn't spotted me yet. I wanted to stay there in that moment, one where I had the potential of having a father who loved me, before he could say anything to ruin it. I didn't want my image of him to change. I didn't want his love for me to be tainted by choices made when I was a baby or by his opinion of me now.

He looked up from his phone, and I swear I saw his eyes light up as he stood from the table and rushed over to me. Before I could say anything, he had me embraced in a hug that I'd never forgotten, even though it had been years since I'd had one. I hugged him back, trying to fight the tears that threatened to fall. I couldn't cry the minute I met him. That had to wait until I had a real reason.

He pulled back, holding me at arm's length and taking me in. "Look at you, you're all grown up. I like the red."

I didn't know what to say. Everything I'd gone over in my mind had fallen away and I was left standing there with an empty head with gears that refused to spin. I blinked at him a couple times as his smile slowly faded to a more solemn look.

"I've missed you."

Then why did you leave me?

"I… I missed you too."

He put his arm around me and guided me back to the table where he'd been sitting. He pulled a chair out for me and I sat as he pushed it back in. Then, he took his seat and slid a menu over to me.

"Get whatever you want, my treat."

I wasn't hungry. My stomach was in knots over this meeting, and it only seemed to be getting worse. I'd been hoping that I'd calm down once I saw him, but my body had other ideas apparently. The waitress came up to us all too soon, and I was left gaping at her when she asked what I wanted after taking my father's order.

He looked over at me, placing a hand over mine. "How about a milkshake and a spicy chicken sandwich? It used to be your favorite."

He remembered.

I nodded, and the waitress smiled as she jotted down the order and then turned away to go back inside. Glancing up at my father before staring down at my hands, I fidgeted, my leg bouncing uncontrollably. A thousand questions raced through my mind, but one screamed over all the rest: *Did you let them cut me apart as a baby?*

I didn't want to lead with that. No, we had to wean ourselves into a conversation that deep. God, I wished Theo was here. They'd be grilling my dad, not even giving me a chance to stew the way I was right now. He'd be the one on the defensive, not leaning back into his chair as if he didn't have a care in the world. Why wasn't he more nervous? I'd be crawling out of my skin with guilt, seeing my daughter for the first time in three years. Then again, I wouldn't have left her in the first place.

Me. He left *me*.

I was distracted when his hands came into my view, his calloused, rough fingers engulfing my pale, soft skin in his embrace. "Honey, whatever you've got on your mind, you can tell me. I'm the one who fucked up here, not you."

My gaze snapped up to meet his eyes. He was admitting he did wrong by me. But why hadn't he done anything to change it?

I decided to start with the second thing burning at me. "I'm… I'm not straight, dad."

He leaned back in his chair, taking his hands away from me. I knew it, he'd leave me too.

But his face didn't show the anger that had been my mother's instant response. I couldn't read his expression, it was so neutral, almost more unnerving than the rage I'd expected.

"So what, you've got a girlfriend now?" No judgment in his tone, just a genuine question.

"Not… not exactly. I have a partner, Theo, they're non-binary."

He blinked at me.

"Liz. It's Liz, dad. But they're not Liz anymore."

"Huh." He stared in my direction before slapping his knee. "I always knew that girl had a crush on you, the way she followed you around like a puppy dog."

"Not a girl."

"Right, right. Sorry."

Then came the uncomfortable silence as I stared down at the

table while he looked me over. The waitress came by with our food, and I feigned a smile while my dad thanked her. My dad took a few bites of his burger while I pushed around the fries on my plate, my stomach still too upset to eat anything.

"Are you happy?" He broke the silence.

"With them, yes."

"But not otherwise?"

"Everything's… kinda messed up right now."

"Well, as far as you not being straight, it doesn't matter to me. I just want you to be happy. I'm glad Theo makes you happy. What's messed up about right now?"

I sighed, relieved at his response but also anxious to tell him what was going on, as it would lead to *the question*.

"I'm living with them. Mom kicked me out when she found out."

"Bitch." His face curled into a snarl.

I was a bit taken aback. I'd never heard him swear before today. I'd never even heard him call someone names. I knew my mother's relationship with him had gone sour, obviously, but I'd never assumed he had it in him to call her a bitch.

He must've seen the bewildered expression on my face, because he backpedaled. "I don't mean to call anyone names. But she never should've done that."

"That's not all she did."

He reached over his plate and took my hand again, urging me on.

"She hit me. With a belt. She wants to send me to a conversion camp. And…"

His hand trembled with the rage I'd expected to be aimed at me, but it was all towards my mother. "I'll have her arrested."

"Don't. It's her word against mine, and I don't want Leah going through that."

"What if she hurts Leah too?"

"She won't. She's always loved her more. I know you know it too."

His expression softened, and I couldn't stop what came out of my mouth next.

"Why did you leave me with her?"

He let go, rubbing at his face roughly with his hands. "I shouldn't have, I know that. I took the coward's way out, but I couldn't take it anymore. I tried to get custody, but the lawyers said it was a lost cause, I should just move on."

"Well, you've got a new family, so I guess you took their advice."

"Is that what you think? I didn't replace you, Allie. I could never. I think about you and your sister all the time."

"Then why didn't you try to contact me? It was so easy this whole time."

"I'm a coward. I was afraid your mother would interfere."

Another long pause between us, neither of us making eye contact this time. Eventually, he broke it again.

"Can you ever forgive me?"

"It depends."

"On what?"

"I also found out I have androgen insensitivity syndrome. I'm intersex."

He was silent.

"Mom told me about the surgery they did on me when I was a baby. Did you want it too? Did you just let them cut me up for no reason?"

"It wasn't no reason, it—"

"What, I wasn't good enough for you?"

"No! Not at all, just—"

"Just what?!" My voice was getting louder, and I could feel the stares of a few other people on us as I leaned into the table, anger rising inside me. He was *defending* this decision.

"The doctors made it sound like we had no choice. Like it was something that *had* to be done."

"And you didn't question them?"

"We were out of our depth, they made it sound like a cancer that needed to be cut away, and we trusted them."

I scoffed and rolled my eyes, leaning back in the chair so that my spine collided with the hard iron bars.

"Would you have wanted to be like that? You're so clearly a girl, I don't see what the issue is."

"It's *my* body. I would've liked it to be my choice. You don't have to have a typical vagina to be a girl. It's like I wasn't good enough as I was, and you had to slice me up before I could even understand what was going on. You know what it's called in the intersex community? Genital mutilation. I was *mutilated*."

He sat there, blinking at me for a moment, with a slight squint that alluded to the cogs slowly turning in his brain. I kept my arms crossed, staring down at my untouched food.

Finally, he spoke. "I'm sorry you feel that way, Allie. We thought we were doing what was best for you."

I scuffed my shoe on the sidewalk. "Mom thinks I'm a freak."

"Well, you're not. You're always going to be my baby girl, no matter who you love or what parts you have. I'm sorry we did wrong by you. Knowing how you feel, if I could take it back, I would."

Nodding, my vision blurred as tears forced their way into my eyes. At least he understood. He might not be innocent in the situation, but he hadn't meant to be malicious either. He didn't refer to me as "messed up" like my mother had. I took in a deep breath, and the sobs started as I whispered, "I miss you, daddy."

Rising from his chair, he rushed over to me and engulfed me in his embrace. I leaned into his chest, letting the tears fall, done with forcing them back. We stayed like that for some time, until my tears subsided and I was able to lift my head from the crook of his neck. I wiped at my eyes, sniffling as my dad sat back down across from me.

"I miss you too, sweetheart."

My stomach growled, the knots finally working themselves away. I took a sip of my milkshake and started picking at the now cold, but still tasty fries. My dad smiled and took a couple more bites of his own food.

"We won't go this long ever again. I want you to meet your half-sister, and my fiance. You'll love them. And if you need to, you can come live with us, there's a spare bedroom you can have."

I shook my head, "I like living with Theo."

His smile faded, disappointment covering his face.

"But I still want to meet them."

He beamed. "Okay. The door will always be open for you. Can I meet Theo? I mean, I know I've met them before, but I'm sure they've changed."

I snickered. "You have no idea how much. You can meet them now if you want, knowing them they haven't left from the block away where they stopped walking me, just in case. I can text them."

"They're protective of you, are they?"

I nodded. "Very."

"I'm glad someone's been looking out for my little girl."

Rolling my eyes, I pulled out my phone to shoot Theo a quick text before putting it away and taking a bite of my sandwich. I must've been right, because within minutes I felt a light touch on my shoulder and looked up to see Theo. They looked equal parts nervous and relieved that everything was okay, and I pointed at a vacant table next to us.

"Pull up a chair."

They did, but before sitting held out their hand for my dad to shake.

"I'm Theo, you knew me before, but I'm really different now."

My dad gave them a warm smile, "I'll say. All that hair you had, gone! But this cut suits you I think."

What a contrast from my mom's condescending "You look boyish."

Theo smiled and took a seat, wasting no time in picking at the fries on my plate.

My dad laughed, "Why don't we order you something? Alex has barely started in on her plate anyway."

"Okay, I'll have the same thing as her."

My dad waved the waitress over and put in an order for Theo while I took a few more bites. We talked about school and how shitty everyone was, and he filled me in on his family. I even told him about Theo teaching me to fight, and he dipped his head at Theo.

"Thank you for keeping my daughter safe when I couldn't."

Theo blushed, not used to that type of compliment. Usually their abrasiveness was met with distaste, but in this case it was appreciated.

We continued talking long after Theo had finished their plate, and as the sun started to dip over the horizon, my dad sighed and stood from his seat.

"I suppose… suppose we should get going."

I got up and he pulled me into a hug, kissing me on the top of the head.

"We'll do this again soon. Or maybe we'll have dinner at my house, so you can meet everyone. Theo's welcome too."

He turned and shook Theo's hand again, then threw some cash down on the table as a generous tip for occupying the table for so long.

Just like that, my father was back in my life, and he was everything I remembered. At least I had one parent who loved me unconditionally.

———

Seeing my father had calmed a lot of my nerves and made me feel like I had more of a family looking out for me, but it also created an ache of loss within me. Friday morning, all I could think about was Leah. I missed her so much. She was the only reason I'd put up with my mother for so long, and while it was doing me wonders being away from a mother that held nothing but contempt for me, it hurt me not to see Leah.

So, after Theo, Elliot, and I parted ways for our classes, I passed right by my classroom and went out the back door of the school. It was homeroom anyway, surely they wouldn't call home over me missing one class. Taking in the crisp spring air, I walked the two city blocks over to the elementary school where Leah was enrolled. I walked around the back to a chain-link gate that stood between me and a group of frolicking children. Leah's school always started with recess, something about getting some energy out of the kids before having them hunker down into their lessons. I put my hands up against the fencing, searching the group for my sister's dirty-blond braids that my mom didn't let her leave the house without.

Then I saw her. Taking in a sharp breath, tears instantly began trying to force their way out of my eyes. I rubbed at them, refusing to let the tears fall. A kid playing catch with my sister caught sight of me and pointed over in my direction. Blinking away the last of the tears, I forced a smile as Leah ran over to me, jumping to try and reach the latch on the gate. She managed to get it open on the third try, and wrapped her arms around my waist, burying her face in my stomach. I knelt down, embracing her and rubbing her back.

After a couple minutes, she pulled away, tears in her own eyes. "Why are you here? Won't you get in trouble for missing school?" she signed.

"It'll be okay. I just needed to see you. I miss you so much," I signed back at her.

"I miss you too." She hugged my arm, and I pulled her in close for another full hug.

"Are things okay at home?"

She nodded, "Mom seems… less mad. Maybe you can come home?"

I didn't have the heart to tell her that mom was probably less mad *because* I wasn't there. That me coming home was a terrible idea, for everyone involved.

"I'm sorry, sweetie, I can't."

She pushed out her lower lip and pouted, giving me a puppy dog face I couldn't resist.

"I wish I could."

She kept giving me that damn face.

"Maybe… maybe I can try and come here on the mornings that I have homeroom, when I won't get in trouble."

She perked up at that. "Really?"

"Yeah, I'd like that too."

Bouncing on her toes, she gave me another hug before I saw a teacher wave her over.

I pointed and signed. "You should go, love. I'll come again."

Before Leah could leave, the teacher walked over to us. "Alexandra, is everything all right? Shouldn't you be in school?"

"Y-yeah. Everything's fine, I just really needed to see her."

She raised an eyebrow at me as Leah slipped past her and back into the school building where classes would soon start.

"Please, please don't tell my mom I was here."

The teacher crossed her arms, leaning back on her heels a bit. Teachers usually liked me, but I knew that me skipping class to see my sister wasn't a good look. No one knew that I wasn't living at home, and I needed it to stay that way. So I nervously shifted my weight between my feet as the teacher looked me up and down, trying to assess the situation.

"Please," I begged.

The woman broke her stern expression with a smile. "I'm just messing with you, honey. Who am I to keep a girl from her little sister? You mean so much to her."

I let out the pent-up air that I'd been holding and my shoulders slumped as relief washed over me.

She placed a hand gently on my shoulder. "Don't be so nervous. Really, is everything all right?"

I nodded, "Yeah, it is. I was just missing her today."

The teacher patted me and turned me around, "Good, now get back to class before they miss you."

Waving, I took off down the street back towards the high school. I wished with everything I had that I could take that little girl with me to Theo's, to have her with me all the time. At least now I knew I had the chance to see her a couple times a week.

CHAPTER SEVENTEEN

I awoke alone in Theo's bed on Saturday morning. At first a panic overcame me, but then I realized Dulce was gone as well, so they must've been out for a run. Sure enough, I checked my phone to see a message from Theo that said they were out running. I was glad Dulce was so good for them, they always came back from runs in a good mood. Sighing, I sat up and rubbed the sleep from my eyes, then dragged myself from the bed, rummaging through Theo's drawers to find something comfy. I decided on an oversized hoodie (big surprise) and some leggings that I was pretty sure were mine anyway. Theo never wore leggings.

Making my way to the bathroom, I shut the door behind me and dug through a cabinet in hopes of finding a shower bomb or something similar, I wanted some sweet scents to soothe me. I wasn't in the worst mental state I've been in the last couple months, but I wanted some self-care today. I managed to find a small pack of citrus shower bombs buried in one of the cabinets, and eagerly took one out. Turning on the shower, I undressed and then dropped the bomb as I stepped into the tub. My nose took in the bright scents gleefully, and it helped to wake me up a little.

I relaxed under the stream of hot water – not scalding, but hot enough to work its way into my muscles and relax some of the tension in my body.

A knock came at the door, and I panicked a little, realizing I'd forgotten to lock it. "Yeah?" I called.

"Al, it's me. Can I come in?" Theo's voice was chipper and calm at the same time, undoubtedly a result of their run.

"Oh. Yeah, sure." I relaxed into the stream of water again, hearing Theo click the lock behind them. They must've been really quiet getting undressed, because I didn't hear anything in the room until the shower curtain pulled back slightly and Theo climbed in behind me.

Theo inhaled deeply. "Mmm, you found my shower bombs." Then leaned in and kissed me. They weren't even under the water yet, but they were wet. Sweat. Gross.

I tiptoed around them, effectively switching places so that they were under the water instead of me. "Get the sweat off before you go touching me," I joked at them.

They rolled their eyes playfully, then grabbed a loofa and some body wash and set to scrubbing themselves, then pulled me into them.

I leaned into the embrace, taking in the fruity scent of their body wash. "Much better."

They reached around and placed their hands firmly on my back, dropping the loofa behind us. Kissing with intention, I laced my arms around the back of their neck. I was overcome by the scents around me and the sensations running through my body. Citrus mixed with berries. Steam dampening the air. Tingling heat. Sparks rushing to bodily points of contact. An ache for something more. It all felt so *good*. Theo's hands slowly wandered, and we made the most of our shower together.

Afterwards, we sat down in the tub, breathing heavily as the water continued to rush over us. Theo held me close as we kissed again, not a sign of anxiety in sight. They had a smile on their face as they closed their eyes and rested their head on the back of the tub and stroked my arm. I reached up and held their arm close to me, kissing their hand and then bringing it to my chest.

For a second, I felt their body heave as if they were sobbing, and I looked up in concern. How had it turned sour so quickly? But when I looked up, I realized it wasn't sobs, they were *laughing*.

"What's so funny?" I asked them, a smirk playing at the corners of my mouth.

"This… ha… this was really nice."

"It was. It is."

"I never felt bad, not once. I didn't have to stop at all. Is this what it's supposed to be like?"

"Yes."

They buried their face in the crook of my neck, kissing me and holding me tighter.

"I do like it. Only with you."

————

Later that morning, after we'd torn ourselves from the sanctuary and magical place that was that shower, we were downstairs, sitting at the kitchen island, watching Seth cook. He'd gotten a late start. He was a notoriously late riser on the weekends. We'd been *busy*, so he still had the chance to make breakfast for everyone. Monica was even there, sipping tea at the end of the island while she checked messages on her phone. Jeremy emerged from the guest bedroom, drawn in by the scent of bacon and eggs. He took a seat next to us, rubbing sleep from his eyes as he yawned.

This. This was a family. Not one person in this room was related by blood, but everyone loved each other and was happy to share a meal together. It was a comfortable lack of conversation as we listened to the bacon crackle in the pan and Seth hum as he pulled dishes from the cabinet, laying a plate in front of each of us. Everyone was safe here.

Seth pulled the bacon from the pan and patted off the excess grease with a paper towel, then placed the plate filled with it in the middle of the island. I eagerly swiped a few pieces, dropping them quickly on my plate as the hot grease made contact with my hands. I shook off the heat and Theo laughed at me, scooping their own bacon with a fork so as to not make the same mistake I had. Jeremy picked up his own bacon like he was immune to heat, not even the slightest wince on his face as he brought a piece to his mouth and bit down. Monica set down her phone and took a couple pieces with her fork, the same way Theo had.

Eggs came next, perfectly scrambled to a light and fluffy texture. Then toast popped from the toaster, adding onto a small pile I hadn't noticed Seth making the whole time. A breakfast of champions. Seth sat down on the other side of the island after bringing the plate of toast and some butter and jam over, and we all dug in.

"How's school been?" Monica asked, addressing all of us. Jeremy, Theo and I all exchanged some wary glances, until Theo spoke.

"Shitty. There's a group of kids that hates us, they're constantly trying to start fights. They hurt our friend."

Monica furrowed her brows, "Is the school doing anything about it?"

Theo shook their head, "Guidance counselors don't give a shit. We've just been dealing with it."

Shaking her head, Monica let out an exasperated sigh, "I'll have a talk with the school. That's not okay."

"They won't care. With my track record, they assume I bring on the fights myself. I only defend myself and Alex now, I promise."

"I know, honey. You've been doing so good. I know it's hard."

I perked up, remembering the invitation Harriet had given us. "We made a few other queer friends though. This one girl reached out to us and invited us to hang out after school."

"Are they nice?"

"Yeah! I really like them. T, actually, Harriet invited us to a party instead of prom. She said it's like the queer kid alternative. I know you're not much for the prom scene, but I think it might be fun."

"We can go." They surprised me with their quick response.

"Really?"

"Yeah. Don't expect me to be good at dancing though, I suck."

I smiled and playfully pushed their shoulder. "Jeremy and Seth, you guys can come too."

"I don't have a date." Jeremy said, a little somber.

"That's okay! We can go as a group. I'm sure the others from Best Boba will be there."

His eyes flickered. "You think Elliot will go?"

"For sure. He's in Harriet's inner circle. Why? You like him?" I smirked at Jeremy, eager to egg him on.

"He's... he's really cute." Jeremy muttered. "I don't have anything to wear though."

"We'll find you something! I get to dress Theo too, I'm excited."

"Who said you're dressing me?" Theo side eyed me.

"C'mon, T, it'll be fun. I won't pick anything you don't like."

Theo shook their head, "Nah, I know what I want to get."

"Please tell me it's not jeans and a t-shirt."

"No, you'll like it. I mean, yes jeans, but nice ones. You'll see."

"I suppose I'm paying for this?" Monica butted in, her tone wary.

"Uh…" All three of us exchanged looks. Theo wasn't the money bank they used to be when they were hustling at cards to get drug money.

Monica's face lightened, "I'm just messing. I'm glad you kids have something to look forward to, you deserve it. It's been a rough year. Just don't run the bill up too high."

I couldn't stop the grin that made its way across my face, this meant I could get a nice dress, I was so excited. Nodding at Seth, I asked, "You wanna come?"

"Is it all sophomores?"

"No, it'll be a mix I think."

"Sure, I'll tag along.'"

"Monica, is it okay if we go shopping today? I mean, unless you guys had other plans?" I asked.

Everyone shook their heads, and Monica smirked, then reached into her back pocket, pulling out her wallet. She took a credit card out and slid it across the counter to Theo, making a plasticy scratching sound as she did so. Theo picked up the card and put it into their pocket.

Seth nodded. "I'll hang back, I've already got stuff to wear. I should practice my guitar anyway. I've got a small gig coming up with the band."

"Really? that's so cool!" I leaned in, Seth didn't talk much about his personal life. It always kinda felt like there was a wall up around him. Something told me the distance he put between people wasn't intentional. We often got caught up in our small circle of drama too, it wasn't entirely his fault.

He waved his hand. "Nah, we've played there before. Just a

small open mic at a cafe."

"I still think it's cool. You don't talk much about your band."

He shrugged. "We don't sit down together very often."

"You're right, we should do it more."

Monica smiled, watching all of us chatter about our upcoming plans. We had her to thank for all of it, she had created a space safe enough for all of us, something truly beautiful.

———

Theo, Jeremy and I walked into the huge clothing store at the head of the mall, eager to pick out clothes for our first party together. First, we walked into the men's section, and Theo went straight for the jeans.

"You don't want a pair of nice slacks at least?" I asked.

They shook their head. "Nah, I told you, I know what I want."

The desire to dress them was burning within me, I knew how handsome they could be when they were cleaned up. It took everything within me to not backseat shop.

"Okay, okay, I'll trust you. But I reserve the right to veto."

"You won't, I promise. You'll see. Why don't you help Jeremy? He seems a little lost."

I looked over, and sure enough Jeremy was rummaging through a rack of suit pants with a grimace on his face. Leaving Theo to their own devices, I walked over to Jeremy and put a hand on his shoulder. "Need help?"

"I dunno, just… none of it feels right. I've always hated suits."

"You don't have to wear a suit."

"What else then? Everything here feels wrong."

"What feels right?"

"I don't know, that's the problem."

"Hm." I placed a hand on my chin, thinking while looking Jeremy up and down. He squirmed under my gaze. "Button downs? Vests?"

"I hate them all."

"Why don't we look in the women's section?"

"You think I could pull anything off from there? I'm all lanky and angles."

"Sure you can! Let's go."

Instantly, I took Jeremy by the hand and was dragging him behind me to the other side of the store. He fidgeted nervously after I stopped in front of the vast section of blouses and dresses.

"This feel any better?"

He paused, like he didn't want to admit it. "I like all the colors. And flowy things. I'll look ridiculous in a dress though. I don't have your nice curves."

I scrunched my face a little. "Well, thank you, but you don't need curves to pull off a dress."

Jeremy rubbed at his arms, still glancing around as if he was afraid someone would call him out for shopping in the 'wrong' section.

I wanted to put him at ease, so I stopped and put a hand on his arm briefly. "Why don't you help me pick out a dress first, then we'll do you?"

He nodded, looking a bit relieved. I headed straight for some satiny looking dresses with swooping necklines, while Jeremy looked off in a different area, still careful to stay in line of sight from me. His posture reminded me of a child doing something they knew they weren't supposed to, like he'd be caught and reprimanded by a parent at any moment. He'd always struck me as a little effeminate, but seemed to have trouble coming to grips with it.

Turning my attention away from him, I looked through the dresses. I pulled out a couple black ones, looking them over and putting them up to myself to see how the fit might be. I particularly liked one that had lace sleeves and fell just above my knees and threw it over my arm to try on. Continuing my search, I found an emerald-green dress that was fated to be mine. Theo loved me in green. It had ruffles zigzagging across the front of the dress, with a modest scoop neckline that didn't reveal too much, and the bottom hemline rested above my knees. There was a sash across the waist that you could tie to accentuate any curves. I smiled, putting it over my arm. I still liked the black one, but this one was perfect – I'd try them both on, but the decision was already made in my head. I'd surprise Theo with this one. They'd lose their mind.

Turning around, I stopped short before running into Jeremy, who was standing right behind me. I hadn't heard him approach. He held a white card in his hands with a bit of a chain looped around the back – a necklace.

"I know we were looking for clothes, but I found this and... I think it would be beautiful on you." He turned the card around, to reveal a thin silver chain with a silvery silhouette of a bird with its wings outstretched for a pendant. I took it with my free hand and held it up to the green dress – the silver a perfect accent to the emerald.

A wide smile formed across my face. "I love it, Jer. It's perfect. All I need are shoes."

We wandered through the store to the shoe section, stopping briefly in front of a selection of heels. I looked them all over before shaking my head. "No, I'm already so much taller than Theo. I should get flats."

Snaking our way to the next aisle over, we found an array of sandals. I liked flats so much better than heels anyway. I looked next to me for any indication from Jeremy as to which pair I should go with, when I found him gone. Blinking, I looked around for a second but then shrugged, deciding he must've gotten distracted by something that caught his eye. I turned my attention back to the shoes, and quickly selected a pair of silver goddess sandals with thin straps that went up the ankles. As I pulled a box in my size from the shelf, I felt Jeremy arrive at my side.

"Look at these!" He exclaimed, holding up his own shoebox.

It was a pair of gothic-looking boots, combat-style. There were black straps with silver buckles running up the length of them that ended just below the shins. I knew this wasn't a style meant for me. These were for him.

Smiling, I nodded in approval. "Ooh, I've got *ideas* now."

The tension had fallen from him a bit, he was much more relaxed as he followed me back to the clothing section where I made a beeline towards the skinny jeans. I pulled a black pair that had some rips along the thighs and held them up to his waist before shaking my head. "No. How do you feel about leggings?"

"I've always been too nervous to wear them in public, but I secretly love them."

I grinned. "It's time to break out." I led him deeper into the women's section where we found a huge selection of leggings to choose from. This time, I followed his lead as he took in the vast array of choices before him. He pulled out a pair with a deep purple galaxy print before turning to me for approval. I nodded. "I know exactly what we need."

Leading us back to the jeans, this time I pulled a pair of black denim shorts, barely stopping on our way to the button-down shirts.

"When you said you didn't like button-downs, was that all of them, or just the men's?"

"I like some blouses. I don't like the boxy men's style ones."

I nodded before pulling out a black button down with frilly, short sleeves. He looked a little less pleased with this selection. "Really?"

"Trust me, I've got an idea. Go pick out a necklace and some earrings, you've got good taste in jewelry. Then meet me at the changing rooms."

He took the shirt apprehensively, then turned back to the jewelry section. I found my way to the changing rooms and pulled the curtain shut behind me, hanging up my choices on a hook inside. Sliding out of my sneakers, I pulled my shirt off and then wiggled out of my jeans. I took the black dress in my hands and held it in front of me in the mirror before removing it from the hanger and pulling it over my head. Adjusting the sleeves and lower part of the dress so that it fell in all the right places, I looked myself up and down in the mirror. I wasn't thrilled with what I saw. The dress was fine, but my stomach stuck out more than I felt it should've. At least, I did like the way the lace danced up my arms.

I pinched at my thighs and stomach, ever displeased with my figure. Jeremy said I had nice curves, if only he knew how much I despised my build and how envious I was of his slender frame. Theo always told me how beautiful they found my body, but I didn't see it, ever. My mom's negative comments were what got me really self-conscious. She'd always point out when I gained weight, saying that I needed to watch how I ate now that I was getting older, my metabolism slowing down. After a month of her berating me, I was throwing up after every meal in a desperate attempt to please her. She taught me to hate my body like this. Now it lingered constantly in the back of my mind, and the fact that I simply loved food always worked against me.

I blinked, shaking my head. Shaking away the thoughts that were overwhelming me.

I'm fine, why should I listen to her anyway? This is fine.

Regardless, I had a bad taste in my mouth from this dress. I pulled it over my head as quickly as I could, exchanging it for the beautiful green piece I had my heart set on. Now I was afraid my body would ruin it for me. I put it on, looping the tie around the back of my neck, creating a beautiful neckline perfect for the necklace Jeremy had picked out. Then, I tied the sash at my waistline, sucking in my stomach as I looked down. I looked in the mirror again, trying to quell my inner disapproval of my body, as to not let it taint the beautiful image of this dress.

It was stunning. The ruffles hid all my problem areas, and I turned to look at it from all my angles. Theo was going to lose their mind over this one, the green of the dress perfectly complementing my eyes, contrasting spectacularly with my fiery red hair. I put the necklace and the sandals on to complete the look. I stared in the mirror too long, getting caught up in parts of my body that I didn't like again. This always happened. I wished it didn't. Changing out of the dress, I slid back into my jeans and t-shirt, then put my sneakers back on. I exited the changing room, hanging the black dress up on the return hanger and trying to wipe the scowl from my face. I really did like this dress. I should've been happier, but I was too in my head.

As I tried to shake the thoughts from my mind, Jeremy emerged from an adjacent changing room wearing his outfit, looking apprehensive as if he'd had the same argument with himself that I had.

"I still don't know about this shirt," he said, pulling at the bottom hemline as he looked at me.

"That's because you're wearing it wrong." I handed him my items, then set to work unbuttoning the shirt on the bottom.

Jeremy looked around nervously as I undid the bottom two

buttons, then tied the bottom of the shirt, revealing his midriff. Then, I unbuttoned the top few buttons so that the shirt created a deep V down to the middle of his chest. Revealing the long silver and black chains he'd selected.

"Much better," I said, taking back my clothes.

He looked stunning. The leggings accentuated his long, willowy legs, meshing perfectly with the black boots and shorts. He'd also selected a pair of dangly silver cross earrings that looked perfect on him. He might've been jealous of my figure, but damn, was I jealous of his. He looked in the mirror right outside the changing room, staring, then pulling his hair out of its bun and letting it fall to his shoulders.

I swear I saw a tear in his eye as he glanced back at me with a smile. "I love it, It's… perfect."

Setting my clothes down on a stool next to the mirror, I pulled Jeremy's hair back from his face. "We should get Theo to braid your hair, it would be gorgeous. Rachel was right, your hair is really nice."

He blushed, running a hand through his silky mane. "It's pretty much the only thing I like about myself."

"Wow, Jer, you look amazing." Theo's voice startled me as I saw them come into view of the mirror.

I scrambled to stand in front of the stool that currently held my dress. I wanted it to be a surprise.

Then, I actually looked at Theo, taking in their outfit for the first time. They had a pair of deep blue dark wash jeans on, with a pair of black and white converse. So far, shaping up to be a pretty typical Theo outfit. Their top half sent all kinds of signals to my brain when I got there though. They were wearing the most beautiful deep navy vest with a light filigree pattern on it, over a lavender button down with a skinny navy tie to match the vest. The lavender was the perfect color to complement their skin tone, and the vest cinched around their waist to show off their handsome figure.

I stared at them a little too long, and they burst into laughter. "You didn't expect me to do this good, did you?" They ran their hands down their sides, really feeling themself.

Wanting to kiss them so bad, but needing to hide my dress, I danced between my feet eagerly. "You look incredible. You clean up *so good.*"

They smiled, then ducked back into the changing rooms to swap out their clothing.

Jeremy fidgeted with the knot in his shirt, staring at the floor, having been silent through the entire encounter.

"You still have a thing for them, don't you?"

"I can't help it, my face got so hot when they complimented me. You two are perfect together, I'd never get in the way of that, I promise. I like being friends with both of you."

I placed a hand gently on his shoulder, "It's okay. But you're foolish if you think I'm not going to try and set you up with Elliot at the party."

"Please do, I've got no game."

"Game is tacky anyway. It's the bashful shyness that always wins me over."

"Too bad you're not my type."

I snickered, shoving him lightly as he turned to change back into his own clothes. I took my dress up to the counter, handing the items to the cashier so that they'd be bagged up by the time Theo emerged from the changing room and wouldn't see my outfit.

As if on cue, Theo came up behind me, placing a hand on my lower back as they put their outfit on the counter to be scanned as well. Jeremy came up shortly after, putting his items next to Theo's.

The cashier glanced up at us before asking, "All together?"

Theo nodded, holding up Monica's credit card and swiping it at the kiosk as the cashier bagged the final items. I was too focused on grabbing my bag before Theo could see it to watch the price come up but saw Theo grimace as it flashed on the screen.

"I hope this doesn't break the bank," they muttered, tucking the card back into their pocket.

Jeremy and Theo grabbed their bags, and we exited the store. I felt a rush of excitement come over me, suddenly looking forward to this party even more. I wanted a place where we could just be ourselves, not worry about being heckled or harassed because of who we were. We'd be among friends, ready to have a good time.

CHAPTER EIGHTEEN

The day of the party snuck up on us quicker than we'd been expecting, and I felt an excited buzzing energy as we started preparing Saturday afternoon. We'd all showered, and Theo and I used the upstairs bathroom while Jeremy and Seth shared the downstairs one. My dress was still hidden in its bag, and I was stalling, waiting for Theo to leave the bathroom so that I could get dressed, do my makeup, and surprise them. So for now, I was standing there awkwardly in my nicest set of underwear and a lacy black bra. I put my arms over my exposed stomach and sucked in, getting more self-conscious the longer I stood there. Theo was messing with their hair, trying to get the spiky curls to lay just right on top of their head and smoothing down the sides.

Theo turned and looked at me for a second. "You okay? Why aren't you getting ready?"

I glanced up at them, trying to wipe the sour look from my face. "I'm fine. I just want to surprise you." A half-truth.

They came away from the mirror and walked up to me, pressing their hands against my lower back. "You're going to be stunning, no matter what. But I'll leave so you can surprise me." They kissed me and I reached for the sides of their face, gentle as to not mess up their hair. Then they walked out of the bathroom, closing the door gently behind them.

I pulled the dress from the bag, holding it up to myself in the mirror and staring down at it. Taking in a deep breath, I pulled it over my head and tied the top around the back of my neck, then tied the sash at my waist. Plugging the curling iron in, I pulled out my makeup bag from beneath the sink. At first, I stared at my face, putting my hand beneath my chin, trying to hide what I interpreted as a double chin. I sighed, taking a step back.

Not today. We're not doing this today.

I put some moisturizer on my face, then set to work with the foundation and concealer. I went for a light smoky eye with winged liner and deep red lips. After blending everything together sufficiently, I got out my mascara and watched my blond lashes suddenly appear now that they were coated in black. With the curling iron now hot, I took it to the length of my hair, creating large ringlets that I later split in half to tone them down a bit. I put on the silver bird chain and a pair of dangly silver feather earrings before slipping into the goddess sandals.

One last glance in the mirror, and then I emerged from the bathroom. I was nervous for Theo to see me. I didn't know why. They'd never view me poorly, but still I could feel my stomach churn as I turned the doorknob to their room. Taking in air, I breathed, "T."

They were at their desk, fiddling with a tie clip in the small mirror. Immediately, they turned to look at me. "Oh my god." They stood, practically bounding up to me, and took my hands in theirs while looking me up and down. "You look beautiful."

I felt my cheeks get hot and didn't try to force away the smile that parted my lips. Theo laced their arms around the back of my neck and pressed their forehead to mine, standing on their tiptoes.

"You're always so beautiful. I can't take it," they whispered.

My vision went blurry as a sudden rush of tears tried to spill over. I forced them down. What was I about to cry for?

Theo pulled their head away. "Hey, you okay?"

"Yeah," I muttered, "I just wish I saw myself the way you do."

"Well, start now. You're the most beautiful girl in the world. Believe it."

There was a knock on the door, and Theo and I both jerked our heads towards it. "Yeah?" Theo called.

"Is Alex in there? I need her help." Jeremy.

Theo walked over and opened the door, revealing Jeremy in his ensemble from the store, but a very crumpled looking button down that was all out of sorts.

"I can't get it to tie right. How did you do it?"

I walked over to Jeremy, shaking my head. "You've got it all wrinkled." I went to work, unbuttoning the entire shirt and pulling it down in front of him, trying to smooth out the wrinkles. Then I secured the two middle buttons, leaving the chest mostly open as I had in the store. Taking the bottom bit of the shirt, I tied it neatly, revealing his stomach.

"Thank you," he said, staring down at himself. "You're sure this isn't showing too much skin?"

"You look great," I said, putting a hand on his shoulder, "But you can always button the top a little more if you feel uncomfortable. It just won't show off your chains as well."

"I like it. I've never seen you dress like this, but it really suits you," Theo added.

Jeremy blushed, his gaze landing on the floor. "Thanks," He

muttered, scuffing his foot against the hardwood.

"Jer, how do you feel about makeup?"

"I've never tried it. I have no idea how to do it."

"C'mon." I took his hand and guided him into the bathroom where my supplies were. Rummaging through my bag, I pulled out a deep purple eyeliner I'd never used, along with some shimmer highlight. "I won't overdo it, I'm just gonna do a little and you tell me what you think, okay? If you like it, you can keep this eyeliner. It clashes with my hair. I got it for Christmas one year or something."

"Okay." He fidgeted a little, not looking me in the eye.

I paused, thinking maybe I'd jumped the gun in my excitement. "You okay with this?"

"Ye-yeah… I just. All of this is so feminine, and it's not that I don't like it or that I think it's bad, it's… kinda the opposite of that. What does it mean if everything I've liked about all this is femme? I know I shouldn't feel bad for it, but part of me still does."

With his permission, I leaned in and started lining his eye with a simple cat-eye before speaking, "It could mean a lot of things, but I think only you can really decide what it actually means. You're right though, you shouldn't feel bad about it."

"My mom would kill me."

"I know the feeling. But fuck her. She's not you. Only you can really know who you are." I finished lining his eyes and moved onto the shimmer highlight. I put some along his already well-defined cheekbones and took a step back with a smile. "Take a look."

He leaned into the mirror, inspecting his face as a smile danced across it. "I look… so pretty." He touched his mouth briefly before asking, "Can we do something with my lips?"

"Heck yeah!" I loved doing people's makeup, so I was glad he was into it. Digging through my bag again, I pulled out a deep purple lip tint that matched the eyeliner I'd used. "You can have this too, it's the same deal as the liner. This color looks really good on you."

He turned towards me and I applied the tint, solidifying the punk aesthetic he had going for him.

Theo came to the doorway of the bathroom shortly after, and I waved them over. "Oh, Theo! Do a waterfall braid in his hair, it would be perfect."

Theo pulled Jeremy's hair back over his shoulders as he stared in the mirror, admiring the look I'd given him. "I'm too short for this Jer, you've gotta sit."

He flipped down the lid of the toilet seat and sat down so that Theo could reach his hair, and I watched with fascination as they made quick work of putting his hair into beautiful waterfall braids, one on each side of his head that joined together in the back. I'd never understood how they were so good at braiding, I failed miserably whenever I tried the most basic of braids.

"Okay, now look." Theo patted Jeremy's shoulder.

He stood up and leaned in close to the mirror, as if inspecting every inch of himself. Then he backed up to look at the entire ensemble together. "I'm hot," he whispered.

Theo burst into laughter, while I playfully swatted Jeremy's shoulder. "Yes, you are."

"We ready to get going?" Seth appeared in the doorway. One look at him, and I was stunned. He normally dressed in ripped up jeans and grungy band t-shirts, I'd never seen him dress up in the entire time I'd known him. Now, in front of us, was a distinguished young man in a sport coat and wingtips. He had a floral-patterned button down and then dark wash jeans similar to Theo's. His hair was slicked back, and he wore a single dangly earring. He caught my stare and laughed. "What, too much?"

"Yes." Theo said, giggles still shaking their body.

"I've… just never seen you dress up before." I had the filter that Theo didn't.

"It's… it's the shoes," Jeremy offered, "They're giving wedding, not party."

Seth looked down at his feet, lifting them up one at a time. "Damn," he muttered, "You're right. I never get to wear these shoes." He disappeared into his room, then came back a minute later with some floral-printed converse that matched his shirt. "Better?"

Jeremy nodded. "You might want to lose the jacket too?"

"C'mon, Theo's got a whole vest and tie on! You're telling me a sport coat is too dressy?"

Jeremy raised his hands, "Hey, keep it if you want, it was just a suggestion."

Seth pushed in front of the mirror, taking a step back to try and get a look of his full outfit. "Nah, I'm good. I can always take it off when I get there if it's too much." He turned to the rest of us. "You ready?"

We all piled into Seth's car, and he drove us across town to be unfashionably early to this party, arriving promptly at 5:30 when the party actually started at 6:00. As we walked up to the door, I looked around awkwardly. If we were imposing, Harriet didn't seem to mind as she opened the door and waved us in. She did a double take, looking at Seth as I realized we hadn't introduced them.

"Hey, I know you! You're in that band that plays after school sometimes."

Seth gave her a pleasant smile as Theo butted in. "He's my brother."

Harriet looked between the two of them for a minute, putting the puzzle pieces together in her head. If she had questions, she didn't ask them. "Oh! Welcome then!"

As we stepped inside, we were transported to a magical realm of fairy lights and pop music. Harriet had really gone all out for this, the entire house was decorated. Paper lanterns, streamers, and sparkly wall adornments were all over the place, replicating as much of a prom vibe as possible without actually being one. The biggest difference, everything was rainbow. Hell, this was better than prom.

Harriet led us into the kitchen where she was still putting together trays of snacks. Elliot and Rachel were there as well, putting cheese and crackers out on some of the trays. Elliot was looking quite sharp in a suit and tie with a satin light-blue button down.

Seth eagerly patted him on the back and turned to look at us. "See, I told you the coat wasn't too much. Look at my man Elliot here. I probably could've went for the shoes too!"

Elliot turned to Seth awkwardly, "Do… do I know you from somewhere?"

Theo took a step in, pushing in between Seth and Elliot. "That's just my overly friendly brother. We don't really interact at school, it's easier to avoid the questions that way."

"Oh," Elliot visibly relaxed and shook Seth's hand.

That's when I caught Rachel staring. It was a deer-in-the-headlights look, like she didn't know what to do in the situation. She was wearing a beautiful shimmery silver dress and strappy flats to match, and was nervously fidgeting with a silver necklace with an emerald pendant that contrasted with her deep brown skin. Her hair was curled into what resembled a very short pixie cut, and her eyes were trained on Seth. There was a look of recognition, but also one of fear.

Seth turned to Rachel, and the minute their eyes met his smile faded for a second. It came right back. He rebounded in a way I never would have if someone was looking at me like that.

"I assume your real name is different than the one I know, is it?" Seth asked, taking a step towards her. There was something there, between them. More than simple recognition.

"R-Rachel," she squeaked out, eyes still locked onto Seth. Watching, waiting for his next move. I was missing a significant piece of whatever was going on here, and the not knowing was killing me.

"Pronouns?" Seth asked, closing the distance between the two of them.

"She/her."

"You didn't have to hide this from me, but I'm not angry that you did." Seth held out his hand for Rachel to take.

Seth was on a mission. He held his hand there while Rachel looked around at the rest of us, as if trying to judge our reactions. Eventually, she took his hand, and his grin widened as he led her out of the room.

Harriet looked dumbfounded, "What... just happened?"

"There's chemistry there, that's for sure." I stared off in the direction that Seth had left with Rachel, then glanced over at Theo. "Do you know anything?"

Theo blinked, squinting a bit behind their glasses. "There was this guy last year that Seth was really into, but they were keeping it on the low. He ghosted Seth after a couple months. Seth was really torn up about it. I never met the guy. Maybe... they weren't a guy after all."

"Rachel started transitioning late last year. She didn't have any friends, or anyone really, at school. Maybe she dropped everyone to try and be herself," Harriet added.

"If that's the case, Seth's a goddamn gentleman," Jeremy muttered.

"Yeah, he's okay by me." Elliot's voice was small.

"He's always had that charm. He makes everyone feel wanted. At least, as long as I've known him." I smiled, turning back to the trays of food that were still only half-prepared since the assembly line had stopped to watch that scene unfold. "Need any help with this stuff?"

Harriet blinked, then looked back down at the trays, "I'd hate to put you all to work, you're here for fun."

"Oh please," I waved my hand at her. "We're early, we basically asked to be put to work."

"Well, if you don't mind. We still have to make the punch and lay everything out on the dining room table."

"Anything fun in the punch?" Theo wrinkled their nose, and I shoved them lightly.

"No, that's part of the deal with my parents letting me have this party. No booze allowed. Sucks, I know."

Theo blushed, rubbing the back of their neck with their hand, "I was just messing. I can make it."

Harriet pointed to the punch bowl and Theo went to work, pulling some ice out of the freezer like they owned the place. I helped Harriet finish putting a fruit platter together and Jeremy helped Elliot lay out the cheese and crackers. The clock chimed six just as we were putting everything out on the dining room table, and a knock came to the door. Harriet rushed over to it, opening the door to reveal Brett and Claire from our meetings at Best Boba. They both flashed smiles as they walked in the door and Harriet turned up the music a little. I glanced around to find Seth and Rachel on the couch talking, Seth with his arm around her. He was making *moves*. I laughed to myself before turning to find Theo.

"If you're gonna set Jeremy up, now's your chance." They gestured towards Jeremy who was embracing his wallflower status with a cup of punch in his hand while fidgeting nervously with the knot in his shirt and scanning the room.

I glanced around to find Elliot in a similar fashion on the other side of the room, a small plate of cheese and fruit in his hand while he fidgeted with his tie with the other. I laughed again. These two were meant for each other. Without a word, I took Jeremy by the hand. He was reluctant to follow at first, until I turned around to give him a slight glare, then he came willingly. Elliot's eyes locked onto us as we approached.

"Elliot, Jeremy, if you're going to be wallflowers, at least do it together." I turned Jeremy so that he was standing side by side with Elliot, then nodded and walked away, leaving them to their own devices. I glanced back briefly to see Elliot smile and gesture towards Jeremy's outfit, and Jeremy blush under what I assumed was a compliment. Mission accomplished.

I found my way back to Theo, and they smiled and shook their head. "You're such a meddler."

Wrinkling my nose, I snickered. "I know. What's the fun in letting them stand in opposite corners all night?"

Theo rolled their eyes. I smiled, leaning into them and burying my face in their neck. More people were arriving now, some people I recognized from school, and others I didn't. Harriet dimmed the overhead lights in the house, letting the fairy lights set the atmosphere. She turned the music up a little more, and soon the house was full of people dancing and talking. This was objectively way better than any high school prom I'd ever been to. Not everyone knew each other, but it was still a safe place. No one was alienated for their identity. There were no stares, no double takes, and absolutely no words of hatred. Everyone was happy to be there. Even Theo felt relaxed against my touch, and they were normally pretty skittish around crowds.

I stood up from leaning on Theo, and pulled them towards the living room. "Dance with me." I beckoned them, and they obliged.

Just as we got into the living room, the song changed to a slow pace, and I smiled as I wrapped my hands around the back of Theo's neck, and they rested their hands on my hips. I pressed my forehead to theirs in the dim light and smiled as they leaned in for a kiss. Running my hands through their hair, I pulled them in close so that our bodies were touching. The music washed over us, and we were in our own little world. Nothing mattered, everything was perfect as it was. We were here together, and nothing could tear us apart. There was no containing our love for each other, for this community, and it touched everyone around us.

We didn't need to say it out loud, we both already knew as we lost ourselves in the dance.

www.ingramcontent.com/pod-product-compliance
Lightning Source LLC
Chambersburg PA
CBHW050847190726
48286CB00007B/2272